Lock Down Publications and Ca$h
Presents

THE BUTTERFLY MAFIA 4

Long Live The Mob

Written By
FUMIYA PAYNE

First Edition 2024

Printed in the United States of America

Lock Down Publications
P.O. Box 944
Stockbridge, GA 30281
www.lockdownpublications.com

Like our page on Facebook: Lock Down Publications
www.facebook.com/lockdownpublications.ldp

Stay Connected with Us!

Text **LOCKDOWN** to 22828 to stay up-to-date with new releases, sneak peaks, contests and more…

Like our page on Facebook:
Lock Down Publications

Join Lock Down Publications/The New Era Reading Group

Visit our website:
www.lockdownpublications.com

Follow us on Instagram:
Lock Down Publications

Email Us: We want to hear from you!

Acknowledgements

All praises to the Most High. When it seems like no one understands or cares, You'll show me you do through unexpected blessings. So again, I just wanna say thank you for being my best friend.

Ca$h... We both know, with or without me, your boat gon' float regardless. So I genuinely appreciate you bringing me aboard.

To my editor, Sunny. Ooh, I be criticizing the quality of my content, as if it isn't good enough. So your enjoyment with this series helped me in a way you may never understand. Thank you, Queen.

Shawna baby... I finished it, love! I hope you're happy with the end result. You already know how much I wish we could talk and I could hear your thoughts. But I gave it my all, which I guess is what matters. Everyone knows you had such a sweet soul, and may your memory live on through the character in this book.

To the reader... If you're reading this, then I guess it's safe to say you've read the first three. Without you there's no me, so I wholeheartedly thank you for joining me on this journey. And if you have any questions, comments, or constructive criticism, you can reach out on Facebook @: Fumiya Payne.

Chapter 1

Downtown Chicago

With Lo-Lo lugging shopping bags in both hands, her and Uno were all smiles as they leisurely strolled along Magnificent Mile. They had visited various boutiques where Uno insisted on paying every penny of her costly purchases. He may not have been clocking coins equivalent to the Butterfly Mafia's, but he did enough to show Lo-Lo he could hold his own.

Returning to their rental, Lo-Lo loaded her bags into the trunk of a cream-colored Tesla. Genuinely appreciative of Uno's unselfish shopping spree, she would later reward him with some lingerie modelling and raunchy sex acts. In fact, the silk scarves she bought were to actually tie him up before using her tongue as an instrument of torture.

"Aye, yo, I gotta piss real quick," Uno lewdly announced as he closed the trunk. "So just wait for me in the car while I run in one of these stores."

Inside the luxury sedan Lo-Lo sat in the passenger seat, singing along to Doja Cat's *Morning Light*. Being spoiled by her man had her juices flowing, and she looked forward to ensuring it was a memorable night. She had a sexual trick up her sleeve that would surely blow his mind, like when she had sat on his birthday cake.

The carefree couple had arrived in the Chi' late last night, with the reason for the trip consisting of both business and pleasure. Uno had a prearranged studio session with his relative and had enticed Lo-Lo with the idea that she'd not only get to see him live in the booth, but that he would cover their every expense. Unaware of Asha being at Harper hospital in ICU, Lo-Lo had readily agreed to join him on the three-day adventure.

Upon Uno reentering the car he lowered the music and turned to address Lo-Lo with a direct stare. "Yo, do you honestly believe in your heart I'm a real-ass nigga? Like, for real doe."

She nodded without hesitation. "I do. And I wouldn't be here if I didn't."

He held her gaze for a minute and ordered, "Look me in my eyes and tell me, 'Uno, I know you a real-ass nigga'."

Lo-Lo slightly drew back and eyed him with an awkward expression; for she had never used that word, not even around the twins. True, she was a citizen of the slums, but there were certain boundaries she didn't feel comfortable crossing. "Uno, I'm not comfortable with using that word. It's not my place."

"Says who?" He countered. "I don't give a fuck 'cause you white, you from the D, my baby. And you just as solid as any one of these other bitches out here, if not more. So I need you to talk to me in the language Uno understand." At Lo-Lo's reluctance to obey, he grabbed her chin and forced her to face him. "Say, 'Uno, I know you a real-ass nigga'."

"Uno... I know you a real-ass man who'll understand I can't use that word. I grew up in the hood, but, baby, I'm not black."

His mouth gradually curled into a pleased grin. "That's my girl." He nodded. "That's my muthafucking Lo-Lo. Look how yo' ass just stood on principle and didn't let me budge you. So, yeah, you might not be black, but you just as thorough."

His statement was like a syringe that injected her with guilt; as it caused her to recall the reneging of her oath to the Butterfly Mafia. There was a time in her life when Lo-Lo would've labeled you a liar had you told her she would one day choose love over loyalty.

Uno was on the verge of pulling off when he dug in his pants pocket. "Oh, I almost forgot," he said, withdrawing a small object and passing it to Lo-Lo. "You left that in the store back there."

Almost certain of what was inside the square, velvet box, Lo-Lo frowned in confusion. She knew for a fact they hadn't shopped for jewelry. When she looked up at Uno who had guilt written all over his face, she put the pieces together and accusingly pointed, "You lied about having to use the bathroom, didn't you? You think you slick."

He held up his hands in innocence. "I don't know what you talking about. You done did so much shopping, you can't even remember what all you bought. But maybe once you see it, you'll remember."

Lo-Lo opened the case and gasped at the sight of a twinkling ornament. It was a white-gold ring with a cluster of stones in the shape of a heart. "Oh my God, Uno." She stared in awe of the Kay Jewelers ornament that was obviously expensive. "It's beautiful, baby."

"Every kiss begins with K," he jokingly sang the store's signature song, then leaned closer to capture her lips with his own.

After sharing a slow, sensual kiss that aroused them both, Uno looked in her eyes and spoke from his heart. "I got you this ring as a symbol of my loyalty. We both know the odds stacked against us, but we got a connection that ain't common. It's people out here who go their whole lives and never hit the lottery. And I ain't talking about the one for money, I'm talking about the one for love. That's shit priceless, you feel me? And I don't know about you, but I ain't trying to throw away no winning ticket, my baby. So I'm saying, I'm willing to go against the grain for you. When it come to Lo-Lo, it's fuck the world. But before I step out on that front line, I need to know if you willing to fight for this shit just as hard as I am."

Lo-Lo returned his gaze with a thoughtful expression and earnestly replied, "Uno, I'd be lying if I said sometimes I didn't feel guilty about being with you. Because my peoples don't approve of this relationship at all. But you see where I am. So while you say you willing to go against the grain for me, babe, I've already done that for you. And it's because I agree with what you said about us having a uncommon connection. So it's like, I'd rather miss the shot than never even shoot the ball. Life is about taking chances. And how can you ever win if you afraid to lose. So to answer your question, I'm willing to protect our ticket with everything in my power."

At the declaration of their deathless alliance, they shared a peck on the lips and a lengthy embrace. But if only they knew that the strength of their alliance would soon be put to the ultimate test.

"So you know I gotta ask." Lo-Lo smiled, inspecting her ring as they drove through downtown traffic. "How did you know what size ring I wore? Because it's clearly too perfect of a fit for you to just have guessed."

Minus a proposal, Uno had slid the two-carat ring over wedding finger. "Come on, girl," he boyishly grinned, "you know I know you like the back of my own hand. I took one look at that lil' ass finger and knew what it was off the *muscle*, you feel me?"

"Is that so?" Lo-Lo challenged. "Okay, well, tell me what size shoe I wear, Mr. Know-It-All."

"Six-and-a-half," he readily answered.

"And my bra?"

"Ooh, that's easy. 34-C. And if it come like clockwork, you gon' start your period the end of the month. Like around the 27th, or some shit like that. So I'ma already be ready to deal with your lil' mean-ass."

She playfully punched his arm and laughed. "Your ass would be mean, too, if you had to deal with these vicious cramps. But I'm saying though, don't be over there acting like you know me all like that, player. Like you just been doing all your homework, or something."

"I mean, you know." He comically stroked his goatee. "That's just what happens when you a good student, you feel me?"

"Oh, so if you the student, then that makes me the teacher, right?"

Stopping at a light, he looked down at her lap, licked his lips and lustfully replied, "It depends on the lesson."

"Why you always gotta be so nasty?" She squeezed her thighs together, as the illicit implication of his statement sent tingling sensations coursing through her clitoris.

Uno suddenly looked down at his own crotch and exclaimed, "Nigga, is you serious? What the fuck I tell your hard-headed-ass?"

Lo-Lo started laughing. "Daddy, who you talking to?"

"Nah, yo, this nigga tripping," he said, angrily unbuckling his pants. Upon pulling out his semi-hard pole through the front opening of his boxers, he looked at Lo-Lo. "You better come get this nigga before I do something to him. I told him earlier to lay his lil' horny-ass down and take a nap, but clearly he ain't listening. So if you ain't gon' come over here and teach him a lesson on disobedience, then I'm a be forced to beat this nigga ass."

"You better not touch him," she warned as she unfastened her seatbelt. "I'm the only one allowed to discipline him. Because all you ever wanna do is choke the shit out of him."

Leaning over into Uno's lap, Lo-Lo lovingly licked the vein that ran the length of his meaty erection. "You missed mama, huh?" She smiled in response to its twitching reaction. "And don't worry, I won't let him hurt you. Now let me put you in my mouth and help you go back to sleep."

At the moisturized suction of her vacuum-like mouth, Uno had to tighten his grip on the steering wheel. *I couldn't ask for a better teacher*, he thought as he fought to focused on the road.

Later that evening, after the couple had returned to their hotel to shower and change, they were en route to the studio session with his relative. In addition to their matching Amiri outfits, Uno sported his Bandgang chain while she flaunted her butterfly medallion.

Located in the city's south loop section, Uno turned into the parking lot of an upscale studio called The Spaceship of Chicago. Accompanied by a caramel-complected woman, Uno's relative was already present. With his thumbs tucked into the pockets of his Polo pants, he had his back against the doorframe of a powder-blue Escalade.

Uno broadly grinned as he exited the Tesla, for it had been over six months since they had been physically in touch. "Wassup with my nigga, B.D. Twan?" Uno exclaimed, throwing up his arms in greeting as he came around the car.

Ungluing his back from the 'Lac, B.D. Twan returned the smile. "Wassup, Skud?"

After a sharp crack of their palms as the two shook hands, they pulled each other into a strong embrace. Despite Twan being several years older, the cousins shared a closed bond that could be described as brotherly.

Following the introduction of their female companions, Uno complimented Twan's sparkling SUV. "I see you done stepped up your whip game. This that Platinum Edition, ain't it?"

With a nonchalant shrug, Twan smoothly replied, "Just a soft dolla, you feel me? But I'm saying, my guy." He reached out to finger the Bandgang chain. "It look like you got my truck around your neck."

They shared a chuckle and another handshake before Twan draped an arm around Uno's shoulder. "Come on, let me show you what the Spaceship hitting fo'."

From a southside section of Chicago known as the Low-End, B.D. Twan was a member of the notorious Black Disciples. Brown skinned, with a head full of waves and well-kept facial hair, his demeanor was as smooth as a bald man's head.

Upon entering the Spaceship, Uno was genuinely impressed by its all-white setting. Even the pool tables were white. To the right of the room was the recording booth, which was spacious enough to accommodate a group. There was a small bar, a lounge area with white leather couches, and a PS5 console that was hooked up to a 60-inch flat screen. This was by far the plushest studio Uno had ever stepped foot in.

As Lo-Lo and Twan's girl, Trina, casually conversed on the couch, the two cousins sipped on Patron and shot a friendly game of pool.

"Six in the side," Twan called his shot before he softly sunk it in. While chalking the tip of his stick, he lifted his head at Uno and asked, "So what's going on, fam'ly? How you feeling? You done brought this thick-ass snow bunny down here. Looking like a young Iggy Azalea and shit."

"Yeah, she a bad mu'fucka, ain't she?" Uno proudly smiled, taking a sip of his drink.

"Nigga, she must be *something*," Twan emphatically replied. "You got the bitch in butterfly diamonds and shit."

Uno laughed. "Nah, it ain't even like that, my baby. She got her own bag. And me being a buck, her shit bigger than mine."

Twan paused on taking his next shot as he was always searching for a new stream of income. "What, she cracking cards or something?"

At the thought of Lo-Lo's position and the problems it presented with his piranha-like peoples, Uno answered in a sullen tone, "Nah, it get a lil' deeper than that."

"What's going on, Skud?" Twan inquired. "What you got on your mind? And if it's bigger than words, I can have a hunnid B.D.'s in yo' city *tonight*."

Although he appreciated his cousin's concern, Uno declined the help. This was a problem he'd resolve on his own. "I'm good, bro, believe me. And if shit ever got out of hand, I know how to find you. But I'm saying though," he sat his stick on the table and downed his drink, "I ain't drive all way to Chicago to shoot no pool. Wassup with this booth, nigga? Your bars ain't up to par, is that what it is? Because I know B.D. Twan ain't ducking no session."

He animatedly laughed in response to the challenge. "Awww, come on Skuddd, you know this shit come natural. Matter fact, we gon' do the shit we wrote later. We finna go in this bitch and come straight off the top. And I'ma let you go first so you can set the tone."

With Lo-Lo and Trina paying rapt attention, Uno and Twan stood in the booth, bobbing their heads to a beat they both liked.

Uno turned to Twan as he caught the beat and rapped, "Real niggas 'posed to eat, but may a rat be anorexic/ nowadays they got no ethics, so I had to switch the method/ and since I got felon's record, can't afford *no* mistakes/ niggas play for checkmate, I'm sleeping in a *chest* plate."

Twan didn't hesitate, "I'll cock it back and let it bark whether it's daylight or dark/ boa I'll throw that 'Lac in park and chop his body right apart/ and anything I mention is nonfiction 'til my last breath/ I ain't been the same inside since my got-damn granny left."

Uno went, "Yeah, I got common sense, but I'm not on that conscious shit that Common spits/ rappers making common hits, yapping bout some common shit/ common shit that got me sick, think I need to vomit lit'/ impact like a comet hit, especially when that chronic lit."

Twan came, "Fuck a trick get me rich, nigga that's what *Pac* said/ made a solemn promise to drop knowledge 'til I *drop* dead/ they say money can't buy love and that ain't what I'm looking fo'/ watch the one you think you love turn out to be a crooked hoe/ so get yo' money, trust yourself, and cut back on that driving deep/ 'cause guarantee one of 'em see they self sitting in your driver seat."

Back and forth they would go until the conclusion of the beat.

"Nigga, that shit was hard!" Twan exclaimed as they shook up and hugged. "We should've been recording. Because that one shit you said was so raw, when you was like, 'Common shit that got me sick, think I need to vomit lit'."

"Nah, for real doe," Uno affirmed. "Niggas gotta stop dropping *literature* in these verses. It ain't all about fucking hoes and killing shit, you feel me? That's why I felt you when you said, 'Cut back on that driving deep, cause guarantee one of 'em see they self sitting in your driver seat'. That was some real shit. Because it usually be the ones you roll with on a daily that hate you the most and wanna take your spot."

On account of Twan having children at home, he soon called it a night and told Uno they'd link back up the following day. "And make sure you got your shit memorized. I already paid the choreographer, so, after we lay our verses, we gon' shoot a mean-ass video."

Escorted to their vehicles by the studio's private security, Uno and Twan embraced before going their separate ways. "A'ight, fam'ly, I'ma see you in the A.M.," Uno said, running a hand over his cousin's waves.

"A'ight, Skud, in a minute. And it was nice meeting you, Lo-Lo." Twan waved. "You the first one he ever brought around, so you gotta be good. But take care of my boy."

When they turned out the parking lot, headed in the opposite direction of the Escalade, Lo-Lo pointed at Uno and teasingly accused, "You think you real slick, too, mister."

He grinned. "Why you say that?"

"I know you told him to say I'm the first one you brought around. Trying to make me feel like I'm special and shit. Like I'm the girl you wanna bring home to your mama."

At the mention of his mother, Uno cursed before retrieving his phone from the center console. "Damn, I forgot I was supposed to call that woman before she went to bed. She had a doctor's appointment today and I wanted to see how it went."

Uno was filled with alarm at the number of missed calls and texts on the screen of his Galaxy. When he skimmed through messages that were mainly from D-Nutty, Uno knew tonight's explicit encounter with Lo-Lo was off, as well as tomorrow's recording with his cousin.

"Wassup, babe, why you looking like that?" Lo-Lo inquired, noticing his strange expression. "Is everything cool with your mom?"

Removing his eyes from the road, he gave it to her straight, with no chaser, "They say your girl, Asha, got shot... and they don't think she made it."

Chapter 2

With her chair parked on the side of Asha's hospital bed, a seated Shawna had her head down as she held Asha's hand and earnestly prayed, "...and I'll start going to Church, I'll pay my tithes, and I'll do whatever else you want me to do, Lord. But please... please make Asha wake up. You know how much I love her and how much I need her. And, God, you already gotta bunch of angels, so please don't take the only one I got. And if you answer my prayers, I promise not to ever ask for anything else."

As she'd done over the past three days that Asha had been in the coma, Shawna ended her prayer, opened her eyes and lifted her head in a nervous hopefulness. But like all the other times, she sagged in sadness at the sight of Asha's continued state of unconsciousness. Having lost count of the pleading prayers she'd sent up top, Shawna began to wonder if her heartfelt entreaties were even being heard.

After Shawna explained to Polaris that she had to go somewhere with Asha, she left the child in the care of Ray-Ray and Kiva. Along with their condolences, they sent Shawna on the way with the assurance that little girl was in good hands.

Shawna tenderly stroked Asha's palm with her thumb, when doctor O'Brien entered the room. Considerably tall, with strands of gray in his slicked back hair, he wore a solemn expression that some could construe as him being indifferent to death.

"You should go home and get some rest," he suggested to Shawna, approaching the opposite side of Asha's bed. "You've been here three days, sleeping in that chair and hardly eating. As a doctor, I gotta warn you that what you're doing is unhealthy."

"I can't leave her, doc. I don't expect you to understand, but I just can't leave her."

"But you do understand she's unaware of your presence, don't you? In fact, she's incapable of knowing you're holding her hand right now. She can't feel you, see you, or hear the sound of your voice."

Returning her attention to Asha, Shawna thoughtfully chewed on her bottom lip before defiantly asking, "How you know she can't hear me?"

"Because I'm a doctor, ma'am," he impatiently answered. "And your friend is in a coma, with minimal brain activity. Listen, I hate to sound insensitive, but whether she awakens is out of your control. And that's why I encourage you to go home and get some test. At this point, there's nothing either of us can do to alter the outcome."

His statements didn't sit right with Shawna and she turned to face him. "I know you're a *doctor*, but I also know you're not God. So, whether she wakes up is His decision to make, and His alone."

"And exactly how long are you willing to wait on this decision?"

"For however long it takes," Shawna firmly stated.

"I see..." O'Brien said, shifting his gaze to the clipboard in hand. After conducting the routine check on his patient, he was leaving the room, when he paused in the doorway and turned to state, "I can see that your friend means a lot to you. And again, I hate to come off as uncaring, but you should be aware that Ms. Kincaid has only basic medical coverage. And per hospital policy —"

"So that's what this is about?" Shawna faced him with fire in her eyes. "You're ready to pull the plug just because she don't got a insurance company you can milk for money? Are you even human?"

"Ma'am, I don't make the rules, I'm just simply—"

"No, I get it," Shawna got up from the chair and began gathering her things. "It's only been three days and you're already bringing up insurance. So, this is clearly about money. You clearly don't care that she's only twenty-one, or that she was shot from behind by some coward in a mask."

The doctor retreated a step as Shawna came toward him, for he'd been informed of Noni's psychotic explosion. But instead of her behaving in a similar fashion, Shawna stormed past him and out of the room.

In tears as she reached the elevator, Shawna repeatedly jabbed at its button. She was anxious to exit the building before she completely broke down.

Seated behind Shawna were two female nurses who observed her from their workstation. They would've known if the patient she visited had passed, so they couldn't help but wonder what could've upset her. Besides faithfully sitting at her friend's bedside, the girl hadn't posed one single problem. But their answer came soon enough, as one of the nurses elbowed the other and nudged her head in the direction of O'Brien who had just emerged from Asha's room. With both nurses being familiar with his direct approach, they could only imagine what he said to send the tearful woman running for the elevator.

While hurrying across the hospital's parking lot, Shawna aimed the key fob at the Denali and unlocked its doors. Upon hopping inside, she threw her purse on the passenger seat, buried her face in her palms and cried her heart out. She felt like this was all her fault. She wasn't as worthy as her friends made her seem. Which was why her own mother abandoned her; why her granny had relentlessly beat her and belittled her; why Puma had met her untimely demise; why Asha lay in a hospital bed with minimal brain activity; and why God was refusing to answer her prayers. She was condemned to a lifetime of pain and suffering and was naive to believe she was deserving of anything associated with lasting happiness. And if others knew the contagious curse of her worthless existence, they'd do well to avoid her at all costs.

After regaining partial control of her emotions, Shawna brought the engine to life and drove off. She was so distraught over her guilt-ridden thoughts, that she made the drive to the MGM without a lick of nervousness.

Double parking by the front entrance, Shawna hit the hazards, hopped out the truck and hurried inside the hotel. As she crossed the lobby with a sense of urgency, Symphony looked up from behind her desk. She wanted to flag Shawna down but was currently on a call with a complaining tenant.

Once inside the suite, Shawna went into the kitchen, opened the freezer and removed a box of ice cream sandwiches and a Stouffer's casserole— both of which she placed in her purse. She was on the verge of closing the freezer door when she reached back in for another box of Stouffer's.

No longer on the phone, Symphony came from behind the desk as Shawna stepped off the elevator. "Hey, what's going on with Asha? I heard that was her that got shot at the gas station the other day."

Barely breaking stride, Shawna replied, "I can't really get into right now, but I'll explain everything to you later."

Still forgetful of the fact she was a nervous driver, Shawna reentered the truck and sped back to the hospital. Receiving directions from the two sympathetic nurses, Shawna found Doctor O'Brien in his office, chewing in a Big Mac.

Wiping his mouth with a napkin as he rose to his feet, he extended his hand for Shawna to take a seat. "I'd like to have a word with you."

She made no move to sit, but removed the boxes of frozen food from her purse and sat them on his desk. "That should be enough to keep you full for a while. Now, if you don't mind, I'd like to go back and sit with my girl. You have a nice day, doctor, and enjoy your meal."

He stared from the doorway to the items on his desk. Unsure of what to think, he picked up a box and shook it which felt to be proportionate to what it reportedly contained. As curiosity overrode caution, he found himself opening the Stouffer's casserole. What he witnessed caused him to open the other two boxes, which both contained the same as the first box.

Dumping the contents of each box out onto his table, doctor O'Brien stared at crisp stacks of cold, hard cash.

In Asha's room, Shawna stood next to the bed, begging her to fight. "I don't care what that doctor say, I know you can hear me. And I'm telling you right now, Asha, you better not give up on me, girl. You better wake your ass up. I need you. I know you think I'm strong and stuff, but I'm really not. I'm only strong when I'm around people like you. When I'm by myself, I be so scared, Asha. And I know I might sound weak, but I can't help it. I would love to be as brave as you, but I'm just not. And Noni mad at me," Shawna sadly continued. "And Lord knows where Lo-Lo at. So, it's just me, and you know I don't like being alone. I love you so much, Asha, and you my best friend in the whole world. So please don't leave me, girl. Because I feel like this is all my fault. Like, if it wasn't for me, this wouldn't have happened to you. So if you can't live, then why should I? When we both know your life is more valuable than mines."

Unbeknownst to Shawna, doctor O'Brien stood outside the room. He'd been about to enter, when he heard her voice and couldn't bear to interrupt such an emotional disclosure. He had worked at Harper for a number of years, and Shawna's plea to the patient was unlike anything else he'd ever heard. Her tone was laced with unimaginable pain, and the rawness of her words were uttered from somewhere within her tormented soul.

While O'Brien's emotions and profession were normally kept separate, he now honestly hoped that Asha Kincaid made a miraculous recovery.

Chapter 3

With the sun on the verge of setting, a pair of Bandgang members sat on the stoop of a house on Six Mile and Martwain. While one of the heathens had a switch-equipped Glock wedged in his waistband, the other had an AK-47 lounging at the toes of his red and white Nike's.

"I gotta let you hear this new shit I wrote last night," the Glock-holder said, then took a lengthy pull from a thumb-size Backwood. As he began coughing up a lung, he held out the blunt for his crony to take.

"That's what your greedy-ass get." He plucked the blunt from his fingers. "I told you this ain't them mids you accustomed to blowing. You gotta hit this shit with class, nigga."

As he brought the blunt to his lips to provide an example, through the wafting smoke he saw a blacked-out Jeep coming up the street. "Aye, yo, yo, yo, check it out, gang," he hastily alerted, dropping the blunt on the porch. "Tell me this don't look like the feds right here."

Aware of the consequences if caught with a 'switch', the cougher stuttered, "W-w what should I do? I got this switch on my shit. You think I should dip right now?"

"Hell naw, nigga!" His crony growled in response. "I gotta muthafucking *assault* rifle by my shit. You might make me hot, and they ain't even on nothing. So let's just see what they do."

Both men's mouths went dry as cotton as the tinted Trackhawk stopped directly in front of them. *I knew I should've ran*, the cougher thought.

The Jeep's passenger window lowered and offered a view of a light skin female. "Aye, y'all know where I can get some trees at?" Noni inquired, poking her head partially out the window.

As their squinting eyes took notice of the blue butterfly tattoo above her left cheek, the cougher and his crony quickly made the connection. This was the notorious Noni of the Butterfly Mafia who their capo, Guru, had intentions on robbing.

"Why, wassup? What you trying to get?" The cougher questioned, while slyly reaching for his Glock. Beside him his crony slowly leaned forward to lay hands on the rifle.

Suddenly extending her right arm out the window, Noni answered his question in the form of rapid gunfire. After a thunderous moment of Martha barking and spitting out print-less shells, Noni donned her hood, hopped out the Hawk and hurried toward the porch.

With liters of blood leaking from holes in his chest, the heathen who reached for the rifle heard footsteps approaching and painfully turned over to eye his executioner. He might've been too physically weak to raise his weapon, but he was morally determined to die like a Spartan.

Noni scoffed in contempt at his courageous reflection. "Take your tough-ass to bed, nigga," she said before aiming at his head and firing twice.

Pivoting toward his partner who laid face-down in a death-like manner, Noni viciously kicked him in the ribcage. "Nigga, you ain't dead!" When he groaned in agony, she ordered him to make eye contact. "You wanna join your boy, or you wanna tell me where that nigga, D-Nutty at?"

Behind the wheel of the Trackhawk, Double-O held a handgun while peering at the rearview for the presence of police. On pure instinct, he looked to his left and saw a man across the street removing an AR-15 from a gray, metal trashcan. With no time to lower his window or open the door, Double-O raised his arm to shield his face and opened fire from inside the Jeep.

On the porch, Noni reflexively flinched at the startling eruption of gunshots. As her attention was drawn to the backwards collapse of her would-be assailant across the street, the heathen at her feet took advantage of the distraction and hurled himself over the porch's banister. He'd prefer a broken bone over a non-beating heart.

Caught off guard by his acrobatic move, Noni fired several missed shots in his direction before leaping over the porch in pursuit. After chasing him through the backyard and now down an alleyway, she extended the gun and let off multiple rounds.

From his forward momentum to the bullet's impact, he did a front flip and fell flat on his face.

Noni caught up to him as he achingly attempted to crawl along the pavement. Barely winded, she pressed her foot on his head and forewarned, "This your last chance to tell me where he at."

"Aye, yo, I can't feel my legs!" he cried in panic. "I can't feel my fucking legs."

She fired a round just inches from his head. "I missed that one on purpose, but the next one I won't. Now tell me where he at."

Shedding crocodile tears and heavily breathing, he told her D-Nutty often stayed with a woman in a duplex over on Dexter.

"You lying to me?" She added pressure on her foot.

He wore a grimace of pain as he swore on his kids he was telling the truth. "But don't leave me back here like this," he pitifully pled. "I ain't have nothing to do with that shit."

"Nothing to do with what?" She asked through gritted teeth, wondering if he was referring to Asha being shot.

"Them niggas trying to rob you. I don't even get down like that."

"*Who*, nigga? Who trying to rob me?"

"D-Nutty and Guru," he ratted them out.

Noni scanned the area, then removed her foot and put him out his misery at pointblank range.

As she cut through the backyard of an apartment building, Noni concealed her weapon before emerging on the next street over. While stepping down the block with her head down, she stuck her thumb and forefinger in her mouth and let out a sharp whistle. She counted to five and whistled again.

It was less than a minute later, when the Trackhawk turned the corner up ahead and curiously coasted. At the engine's sudden roar as the Jeep surged forward, Noni flashed a subtle smirk; for she knew the acceleration was due to Double-O spotting her. *This nigga was worried,* she warmly thought while veering toward the street.

As she hopped in the Jeep and Double-O pulled off, Noni instructed, "Bro, roll up your window."

"I can't, it's gone," he explained without turning. "When I saw that nigga pulling whatever that was out that garbage can, I ain't have time to do shit but shoot through the window."

Noni observed him in fondness as they slowed at a stop sign. "You know this like the second time you done saved my life? If I ain't know no better, I'd say you gotta lot of love for the Noni."

Before Double-O could respond, a cop car pulled up to the corner of the intersecting street; causing him and Noni to stiffen in response.

After several tense seconds that felt like forever, the cruiser sharply turned and stopped within inches of the Trackhawk's grille. "Driver, turn off the car and toss the keys out the window."

Not only had they left behind three dead bodies, but they were still in possession of the actual murder weapons. If booked into the Wayne County Jail, they'd undoubtedly be in a jam impossible to escape.

Wanting to avoid the risk of a high-speed chase, Double-O's clever mind came up with an idea. "Aye, hold on," he warned Noni, before shifting down to 'R' and reversing several feet. Then, shifting back into drive, he sped around the cop car, stopped in the center of the intersection and started doing donuts.

"Boy, you a fool for this one!" Noni grinningly praised, as his crafty move created a cloud of billowing smoke.

Having radioed for backup, the cop couldn't wait to place the driver in cuffs over this reckless stunt. But when the smoke finally cleared— and he was geared up to punch his gas pedal in pursuit, the cop looked around in sheer disbelief. Besides circular tire tracks that stained the street, the blacked-out Jeep was nowhere in sight.

***

As the back bumper of the Trackhawk cleared the entrance of a large garage, two men looked around and quickly lowered its door. While this was mechanic shop by day, at night it served as the city's main chop shop.

Upon Noni unfolding herself from the passenger seat, she was approached by a dark, bald, bearded man who was the size of a grizzly bear. "Wassup with the Mob?" he greeted, cleansing his hands with a torn T-shirt.

"You see it," she replied, dapping him up. "And you?"

Toney-Man shrugged, "A man can't complain if he still breathing, you know? But clearly you ain't here for no counseling session, so how I can I help you?"

Noni nudged her head at the Trackhawk. "That muthafucka hotter than fish grease and trying to swap it out. It's missing the driver side window, but that's it."

Mentally doing the math on a supercharged Trackhawk, he knew it wouldn't be hard to unload it for at least $50,000. "What you trying to get for it?"

"Something just as fast."

He led her past a variety of vehicles before pausing at one that was covered with a black tarp. "I call this one here... Luci." He turned to inform her with a wicked smile. "And I can guarantee you he'll outrun a scalded dog."

When he unveiled the two-door car, Noni groaned in approval at the muscle-bound body of a red Dodge Demon. "This a mean muthafucka," she stamped while circling the American-made machine. And as she came to a standstill at the sinister looking grille, she suddenly knew the nickname Luci was short for God's arch enemy— Lucifer.

"So what we doing, a even trade, or what?" Noni asked.

He pretended to consider her proposal before bobbing his head. "Yeah, we can do that. But only because it's you, and I can't ignore our business in the past."

While a Dodge Demon was a six-figure car if purchased from a dealership, Toney-Man had acquired the car in question through illegitimate means for a measly ten grand. So after he replaced the window and changed the vin numbers, he stood to make a $40,000 profit.

Fetching the car keys from his office, he returned to present her with two different key fobs. "This the standard one." He handed her a black key fob. "But this one here..." He held up a red key fob and cautioned, "This the one that'll turn him into Luci. And unless you ready to meet your Maker, I suggest you respect his power."

Noni summoned Double-O with a wave. As he exited the Jeep and walked up, she extended her hand toward the Demon. "Meet our new friend, Luci."

As Double-O mistakenly assumed an introduction meant him claiming the wheel, Noni loudly cleared her throat. He looked back and asked, "What, I ain't driving?"

Noni cocked her head and just looked at him, to which Double-O released the door handle and made his way around to the passenger side. He knew Noni well enough to know that her look had implied, 'boy, if you don't quit playing with me'.

Shaking Toney-Man's hand in farewell, Noni expressed her gratitude and encouraged him to stay dangerous.

"Likewise," he replied, then offered his condolences in regard to Asha. "And just know I'm praying for y'all."

With one foot in the car, Noni looked back and psychotically smiled. "It ain't us you need to pray for."

Toney-Man could only nod at her indirect message, as he had firsthand knowledge of her infamous history. If her plan was to engage in a citywide purge, then the morgues were in store for an increase in business.

Unafraid of the Devil, Noni ignored the man's warning and inserted the red key fob. She shivered in excitement as the supercharged engine came awake with a growl. Once she reversed out the garage and turned the car around, she connected the Bluetooth and searched for a song. When *Can't Stop* by Skilla Baby began playing, she looked at Double-O and they shared a moment as this was one of their favorite songs.

"It's so hard to stay out my feelings/ no Perc's, still a super gremlin/ it's so hard for us to stop killing/ when you coming from that murder Mitten..."

When Noni turned out the shop and punched the gas, the Demon screamed as its front wheels literally rose up from the ground. With three victims down and many more to go, Noni and Double-O were en route to the duplex on Dexter. It was D-Nutty's turn to take a dirt nap.

Chapter 4

While parked down the street from the duplex in which D-Nutty allegedly laid his head, Noni chuckled to herself at having a sudden thought. "Bro, you know we hot as fuck right now? We supposed to be sliding on some discreet shit, and we out here in this bright-ass car. This nigga probably watching us out the window."

"Sometimes being in plain view is better," Double-O reasoned. "I mean, just think about how many people overlook what's right in front of them. I think energy is what matters the most."

"Energy? What you mean by that?"

"Like, if somebody moving on some nutty, nervous type shit, then that's what they gon' attract. A dog chase you when it senses fear. The police get on your ass when you look back or look away. And people pay attention to you when you look suspicious. So if you can maintain your composure, then I feel like your energy ain't gon' give off no weird vibes, and mu'fuckas will look right past you."

Noni chewed on his spiel and eventually admitted, "Bro, I ain't gon' lie, that lightweight just made a whole lot of sense. You be playing the humble role, but you really gotta strategic-ass mind up in that nappy-ass head."

Double-O was unfazed by her joke but so appreciative of her praise. Growing up, his mother made sure to remind him he was good for nothing, which after a while he began to believe. So to hear the compliment from Noni meant a lot to him.

It was near midnight and Noni doubted that D-Nutty would ever appear. "This nigga probably know we on his ass and he laid up at another woman spot."

Having the patience of a preschool teacher, Double-O replied, "If he ain't in there, he gon' eventually show up. And if he is in here there, he gon' eventually come out. Until then, we just wait."

Through a conversation with Shawna after Asha got shot, they learned that Shawna saw Mecca just moments before the shooting. Aware of how Mecca was a master at puppetry, Double-O recalled the secret meeting between CJ and D-Nutty at the 7-Eleven that night. It was then he told Noni the reason behind CJ's murder, as well as his suspicion of the Bandgang being involved with Asha's shooting. And though he was certain it was Mecca pulling the strings, Double-O convinced Noni it was best to first track down D-Nutty as the right amount of pressure could make a deaf-mute talk.

Two hours later, Noni loudly sighed as she readjusted herself in the seat. "Man, where the fuck is this nigga at?"

***

On the opposite side of town, a black delivery truck rode down a street and stopped in front of a one-story house. Seconds later its backdoor rose and a raid team soundlessly hopped out and advanced toward the trap house. Coming down the sidewalk were two drug addicts, who immediately turned around and scurried off.

Once the house was surrounded, a masked member of the team shouted, "Detroit police! Detroit police!" then he and another man slammed a battering ram into the front door. Upon realizing it was reinforced, they retreated as two others on their team fired teargas through the barred front windows. If they couldn't get in, they'd force the suspects out.

The front door came open minutes later and three young males filed out the house, with their hands up while coughing and choking. After being slammed to the ground and secured in cuffs, they were picked up and led to awaiting patrol cars.

Witnessing the action from a car down the street was a dark-skin man and his passenger, D-Nutty. Both draped in black and wearing leather gloves, they had been on scene before the raid team arrived.

D-Nutty had learned through CJ that the Butterfly Mafia ensured their trap houses were virtually impossible to penetrate. But, determined and desperate, D-Nutty had come up with a way to get inside. Everyone knew that after the conclusion of a raid and a search of the house, authorities did nothing to secure the premises. The doors were left wide open for anyone to enter. So D-Nutty had orchestrated the raid by making an anonymous call to police and informing them that two murder fugitives were hiding out inside.

As he sat back and basked in the success of his plan, D-Nutty knew it was only a matter of time before the authorities left. But unable to recall if CJ had told him the number of people who usually worked the spot, he warned his accomplice of possible danger. "They keep some type of trapdoor in this mu'fucka, so it might still be a nigga in there. Because they can't—"

"How you know all this shit?" his accomplice interrupted.

Angered more by the interruption than the frivolous question, D-Nutty snapped, "Nigga, don't ever cut me off while I'm talking! Like I'm a bitch-ass nigga, or something. Fuck wrong with you? And it don't matter what I know or how I know it, just long as I know."

"My fault, big homie," the younger man apologized. "I ain't mean nothing by it. I was just curious, that's all."

"Nigga, curiosity killed the cat. Now, do you wanna ask questions or put some bread in them broke-ass pockets?"

"You already know."

"A'ight, then. So worry about the nigga that might still be up in this bitch with a sawed-off. Because I ain't come this far to fumble the bag on no goofy shit."

It was near 5 a.m., when the last of Fugitive Task Force vacated the premises. Quickly disengaging the safety of his stainless-steel semi, D-Nutty pulled the hood over his cornrows and barked, "Come on!" before hopping out the car.

Slyly scoping the block as he approached the house, D-Nutty told his accomplice to post up out front while he went around back. "Just in case a nigga try to run. And don't hesitate to shoot."

With his heartbeat pounding from the rush of adrenaline, D-Nutty gripped the gun in both hands as the barrel led the way. Leaning against the house once he got around back, he braced himself for a gunfight, swiveled into the open doorway and was relieved to discover an empty kitchen.

As he quietly entered the house, his alertness alerted him of a movement to his left. It was the refrigerator, which was slowly being pushed away from the wall. *That nigga CJ wasn't lying*, he thought as he positioned himself at an angle of advantage. Whoever it was assumed authorities were gone, and D-Nutty was emboldened by having the element of surprise on his side.

When a frail figure emerged from behind the refrigerator, it was 17-year-old Teer— whose eyes reflected fear at seeing the gunman in the kitchen. Teer's first thought was to run, but he made the mistake of glancing at the back door.

Before Teer had a chance to turn into a cheetah, D-Nutty fired and gave him one of his famous leg warmers. As Teer hollered out and collapsed from the shot to his knee, D-Nutty stood over him and coldly stated, "That was just to stop you from running. Now tell me where it's at, or I'ma stop you from breathing."

The man wasn't wearing a mask. So as much as Teer didn't want to accept it, he knew his journey would end right there in that kitchen. And as he thought about his loyalty-based bond with Double-O and the twins, he fought off his fear in refusal of dying a dishonorable death. The man would take his life, but it wouldn't include his integrity.

As a set of tears slid down Teer's whisker-less face, he eyed D-Nutty and spat, "Fuck you, nigga! And my cousin gon' kill your bitch-ass, I promise you."

"Not before I kill you first," D-Nutty replied before ending Teer's life with two head shots.

Peeking around the refrigerator, D-Nutty took in the trapdoor and wondered if someone was in there, hiding. *Why risk it?* he reasoned, then issued a bird-like call that was used among his crew.

When his accomplice soon stepped foot in the kitchen, his attention was drawn to Teer's lifeless body. The boy looked like a baby.

"He thought it was game," D-Nutty defended his devilish deed. "And I don't play with my own kids, let alone someone else's. But check it out," he motioned for his accomplice to come closer. "You smaller than me, so I need you to go in here and see what he hid."

Approaching the trapdoor in uncertainty, the accomplice knew his size had nothing to do with him being sent into the mysterious contraption. But D-Nutty's merciless reaction to killing a kid made him comply.

As his accomplice entered the trapdoor in a crouched position, D-Nutty was careful to keep him engaged in conversation. It was hard to focus on pocketing things while holding a steady conversation; something D-Nutty knew from his own grimy experiences.

The accomplice reappeared in the doorway a minute later and tossed out a Nike gym bag. "That's all that was in there, " he assured D-Nutty, stepping out and dusting off his clothes.

Anxiously unzipping the duffel, D-Nutty reached in to rummage through Ziplock bags of drugs and stacks of rubber-banded money. Because Noni and Double-O hadn't been doing their daily pick-ups, D-Nutty would walk away with almost $30,000 in cash.

"A'ight, come on, let's— " D-Nutty's words trailed off as he found himself staring down the barrel of a Beretta.

"Drop it like it's hot, nigga," her accomplice advised him with his weapon extended in two steady hands, "and toss your strap on the floor."

D-Nutty couldn't believe his luck. He had made the costly mistake of underestimating his younger accomplice. And as much as he wanted to make a move, he knew it might likely be his last. So, instead, he began frantically thinking on how to get out alive.

"Damn, my baby." D-Nutty smiled in disbelief. "This how you really gon' do me? I thought being Bandgang made us brothers?"

"Nigga, where all that same energy at from earlier? And I'm just doing to you what you was gon' do to me. I'm hip to your maggot-ass. Now throw that strap over there and toss that bag over here."

D-Nutty was on the verge of complying, when he cowered from the crackle of sudden gunshots. As his wide-eyed accomplice fell face forward, D-Nutty caught sight of a hooded shooter in the living room. He let off a few wild shots and took off out the back door; feeling the breeze from the bullets that whizzed past his head. This robbery had turned out to be a lot more difficult than he expected.

The hooded shooter was Double-O, who stopped in his tracks as he entered the kitchen. Lying in a pool of blood was his first cousin, Teer. And judging from the lifeless look in his eyes, Double-O knew it was pointless to call the paramedics.

As he bent to lower his cousin's eyelids, Double-O bowed his head and sought Teer's forgiveness. "I'm sorry, cuz. I got here as fast as I could... but clearly it wasn't fast enough."

When the raid team had rammed the front door, it was then Teer had gathered up the drugs and money and went inside the secret contraption. After waiting for hours while hoping neither of his men revealed his location, he had texted Double-O with a message to come get him.

Having heard all the gunshots from outside in the car, an armed Noni cautiously appeared in the kitchen. Her heart dropped at the visual of her favorite little buddy, stretched out in blood. And for some reason her mind recalled the flirtatious remark Teer had made on her birthday. *Damn!* she cursed to herself, wondering how much pain could a person sustain before going insane.

His expression blank, Double-O rose and wordlessly exited the kitchen. Not knowing what she should say as he walked past, Noni took one last look at Teer and followed her friend out to the car.

They were riding in silence, when Double-O heatedly announced, "Yo, I swear when I die, I hope go wherever that nigga CJ at. Because I'm killing that bitch-ass nigga again!"

This was Noni's invite to inquire what had happened inside the house, to which Double-O explained how he walked in on two men who had been in a standoff. "So I'm guessing these niggas turned on each other, on some greedy shit. But I blow the first nigga down, and that's when I see the other one, holding the duffel bag. Aye, I swear on my *soul*," Double-O gritted while gripping his gun, "I'ma do this nigga, D-Nutty, something bad. I'm a fire this nigga ass up for *real*."

Not only did Noni believe him, but she thirsted to join him on the murderous mission. With her twin reduced to a vegetable-like state, violence was all that made living worthwhile.

"I think that raid was bogus," Noni suggested as she steered them through the city. "How else could them niggas have just popped up right after it? They probably called the police with some wild shit, then waited for them to leave."

As Double-O admitted her theory made sense, they turned back on to Dexter and drove toward the duplex. It was time to get some answers from whoever was inside.

Noni intended to park around the corner, until she saw a woman exit the bottom floor apartment. Her intuition said this was D-Nutty's girl. But even if it wasn't, the woman would know who lived in the upstairs unit.

When Noni double parked the Demon and hopped out with a dangerous-looking Double-O coming around the car, the woman took in the pair and slowed her steps to an apprehensive halt. She considered running back into the house but cancelled the idea at the thought of her children.

Noni waved a friendly hand at something, to which the woman turned to see her youngest child, looking out the window and waving back. "Is that your little boy?" Noni asked as she came to stand before the woman.

She crossed her arms in a defensive gesture. "Why, wassup?"

"D-Nutty," Double-O spat, eyeing the woman in coldness. "Where that nigga at? Because if I can't get to him, I'm settling for loved ones."

The woman looked to Noni for help. "Me and Darnell ain't even close like that. Girl, I'm just working two jobs and trying to take care of my kids. I don't know nothing about what he got going on out here in these streets."

"When the last time you heard from him?" Noni asked while watching her closely.

The woman's eyes darted left before she lyingly answered, "I don't know, it's been a minute. Probably like two weeks ago."

Noni smirked. "Either you think we playing or that nigga got a dick that nut out diamonds."

When the woman opened her mouth to utter more lies, Noni cut her off. "Just let me see your phone. And if you do anything other than pull that bitch out, I'ma put you to sleep and get it myself."

She reached in her purse and withdrew it with attitude. "Here."

There was a sharp crack as Noni viciously slapped her. "Now unlock it."

The woman felt like her cheek was on fire as she unlocked the phone and humbly handed it to Noni.

After reading through recent text messages, Noni returned the phone. "See how simple that was. And if that nigga call you and you tell him we was here, you better move out the state. And I'm BFM Noni, in case you don't know." As the dynamic duo hopped back in the Demon and sped off, Noni looked at Double-O and sang music to his ears. "I think I know where that nigga at."

Chapter 5

Harper Hospital

Shawna was still dutifully stationed at Asha's bedside. Courtesy of doctor O'Brien, she'd been given a bigger and more comfortable chair which likely contributed to her currently being curled up and softly snoring.

Her eyes suddenly popped open as she jolted awake. "Shit," she cursed, rubbing her eyelids and wondering how long she'd been asleep. Returning to an upright position, she now suspected the motive behind O'Brien's hospitable move. Since he couldn't convince her to go home and get some rest, he had rocked her to sleep with the soft-cushioned chair.

Upon directing her attention to the head of Asha's bed, Shawna gasped in shock as if seeing a ghost. She didn't know if this was a pinch me moment or not, but what she did know was that Asha's eyes were focused on hers.

With her heartbeat on the brink of bursting out of her chest, Shawna softly spoke, "Asha, are you looking at me right now, girl?"

When Asha slowly nodded in response, Shawna teared-up and squeezed Asha's hand. "I can't afford for this not to be real," she shook her head back and forth. "So if you really looking at me, I'ma need you to prove it. I don't know, maybe you can blink twice, or something."

Asha blinked twice and Shawna's tears began falling. "I know I'm asking a lot, but do it again, Asha, please. Just so I can be sure."

She did her one better and repeatedly blinked, to which Shawna jumped up and began celebrating like she had just hit the lottery for millions. After crediting the recovery to the merciful Creator, Shawna hugged Asha in her arms and lovingly scolded her, "Ooh, you had me so worried and scared. You should be ashamed of yourself for putting me through that. And don't you ever jump in front of no gun like that again. What's wrong with you, girl? What was you thinking?"

Asha painfully groaned at Shawna's fierce embrace. "Oh my God, oh my God!" Shawna shrieked in panic, gently laying Asha back down on the bed. "I'm sorry, love. I just got so carried away that I —"

"What's going on in here?" A female nurse stuck her head in the room. When noticing the patient had awakened from the coma, she didn't wait for an answer and rushed to get the doctor.

O'Brien arrived moments later and asked Shawna to wait in the hallway. Beneath his composed demeanor was actual joy, as he had been genuinely rooting for Asha's recovery. He just now had to assess the extent of her improvement, relating to physical movements and brain wave efficiency.

Shawna restlessly paced outside Asha's room, when one of the nurses waved her down to their station. "I heard the good news about your friend," she smiled up at Shawna. "And I just wanted to say, I don't think she could've had a more loyal supporter."

"And I don't know how you did it," the other nurse chimed in, "but you even managed to make O'Brien more human. You got the aura of an angel, Chile, and something tells me God got a special purpose planned for you. So don't let nobody tell you different."

As Shawna appreciatively took in their encouragement, she saw Doctor O'Brien exit Asha's room and quickly excused herself. He was pleased to inform her that not only was Asha breathing on her own, but that he expected her to eventually make a full recovery. "However, due to her back injuries, it may be a while before she can walk unassisted. But outside of that, she seems to be just fine."

"Can I see her, doc?" Shawna pled for permission.

O'Brien smiled. "Something tells me I couldn't stop you if I tried. But I gave her a strong sedative for the pain, so you better hurry before she falls asleep."

Shawna eyed Asha in amazement as she returned to her bedside and reached for her hand. "You're really alive."

With the tubes removed from her nose and mouth, Asha was able to hoarsely reply, "You said I was like Tupac, remember?"

"Girl, I was talking about your character!" Shawna exclaimed. "I didn't mean for you to go and get shot five times like him."

After they had a light laugh which earned Asha pain, Shawna continued in a more serious tone, "But for real, Asha, there ain't a word in the dictionary to describe how I grateful I am right now. It's like, I didn't realize how much I loved you 'til I thought I had lost you. Girl, I couldn't eat, sleep, or nothing. All I could do was worry and be scared. Worry that you wouldn't wake up and be scared of the idea of going on without you. And I already know you gon' say I can make it on my own, but it's so much better when we're doing it together. You know what I'm saying, girl?"

Asha laid a hand over Shawna's in a gesture of affection. "I know exactly what you're saying. But Shawna, can you do me a favor?"

"Anything," she readily answered.

"I need you to go take a bath."

Shawna laughed in embarrassment, raising her arm to get a sniff. "Ooh, I do stink. I just couldn't bring myself to leave for even a second."

At the mention of Shawna's continuous presence, Asha inquired about Noni's whereabouts. It would've been nice to see her sister in the room upon returning to life. And it made her kind of sad that Noni wasn't there. Had it not been for Shawna she would've woken up alone.

"This was too much for her, Asha," Shawna offered in Noni's defense. "That girl lost her mind when she saw you in this bed. They had to call security and everything. It literally took for Double-O to pick her up and carry her out of here."

Asha could imagine the tantrum her sister had thrown. And she could also imagine what Noni was doing to cope with the pain. As she could feel herself succumbing to the effects of the sedative, she asked Shawna for another favor before falling asleep. "Go get my little baby and bring her back to me."

***

Not far from the hospital was the Greyhound station. As passengers boarded the bus that was headed down south, its overweight driver was stuffed behind the wheel, busily texting on his phone. Exchanging X-rated messages with a woman he'd just met, the goofy was grinning as she agreed to link up when he returned to the city which just so happened to fall on his payday.

"Aye, man, won't you put that damn phone up and let's go!" A middle-aged man barked in impatience. "Can't you see all the other buses is gone."

The driver held up an apologetic hand and brought his explicit exchange to a temporary close. Returning the phone to his shirt pocket, he went to pull off and stiffened in fear for what appeared to be a terrorist stood in front of the bus, with the barrel of gun aimed at the windshield.

Fed up with the bus driver's insolence, the middle-aged man got up from his seat with the intent on confronting him. But as he marched up the isle and saw the ski-masked gunman planted outside, he quickly changed directions and hurried to the back of the bus— where he locked himself inside the small bathroom.

When a lone passenger curiously leaned over to peer down the aisle at the middle-aged man, the inquisitive face belonged to D-Nutty. Alarmed by the man's fearful expression as he scurried past, D-Nutty wondered if authorities had snuck on the bus. *They gon' have to kill me*, he resolved to himself, reaching for the weapon beneath the magazine beside him.

"Oh my God, look!" A woman pointed in panic, prompting others to stand and take notice of the gunman's threatening presence.

Using a slender white stick as a guide, a blind man in shades nervously tapped his way down the aisle in search of a safer place to sit. When he accidentally tapped the sole of someone's shoe, it was D-Nutty's voice that warned him to watch where he was going. The blind man paused to apologize, and several booming gunshots suddenly rang out.

As D-Nutty was hurled across the seat by hollow-point projectiles, the sound of gunfire ignited a stampede, with people pushing and shoving to exit the bus.

In midst of the surrounding chaos, the blind man removed his right hand from his damaged jacket pocket and revealed a smoking revolver. He leaned closer to D-Nutty and lifted his shades, for the imperative purpose of facial recognition. Some kills were personal, which required the victim to know who was ending their life.

Reflecting a terrified expression as he coughed up blood, D-Nutty stared into the eyes of a coldblooded killer— Double-O.

"This for Teer, nigga," Double-O snarled as he lowered the shades, then stood up straight and fired seven shots into D-Nutty's head. Leaving the print less pistol behind for police, as well as what D-Nutty had taken from the trap house, Double-O jogged down the aisle and hopped off the bus.

As the terrorist, Noni, led them from the area in a stolen minivan, Double-O gazed out the window in deep thought.

His mind had already moved on from D-Nutty and migrated to Mecca. Caressing the hair-trigger of a Glock with his thumb, he wondered what the woman was doing in that exact moment.

Flint, Michigan

With a pair of tinted frames protecting her eyes from the sun, Mecca emerged from a hair salon called Ladies First which sat in the center of a large shopping plaza. Widely known as the best shop in the city, Mecca and her sister, Unique, owned the high-class establishment.

Cautiously scanning her surroundings as she stepped through the parking lot, Mecca approached a candy-orange Cutlass on 30-inch wheels and climbed into its passenger seat.

"Wassup with Mecca?" Hotrod grinned, revealing a Rolex on his wrist as he reached to give her dap.

Bumping his fist in reluctance, she sarcastically replied, "When I said I wanted to meet you, I didn't want the whole city to know."

Confused by her statement, Hotrod frowned. "But I ain't tell nobody I was coming to see you."

"Nigga, that's because this car doing it for you!" Mecca pointed out. "Just look around. You don't see nothing else like this in the parking lot. So clearly this bright muthafucka gon' stick out. And you ain't even got the sense to slap some tint this shit. You might want the attention, but I don't. So don't ever pull up on me in no shit like this again."

While squeezing the wheel, Hotrod's jaw muscles flexed in fury; for his own mother didn't address him with such a hostile tone. But Mecca wasn't his mother and could truly care less about his fragile feelings.

"I didn't hear you," she said at his failure to acknowledge her terms.

Hotrod sassed in return, "That's because I ain't say shit."

As a woman with a low tolerance for the opposite sex, Mecca believed the average man behaved better when on a tight leash, and that the slightest slack often led to unruly habits. So it was important to immediately nip new issues in the bud.

"Let me make myself clear, because clearly I haven't already." She turned to give Hotrod her full attention. "Don't you ever let your mind think for one *second* that I'm one those ratchet, broke-ass, busted hoes you use to dealing with. Nigga, I'm a matriarch. And if you don't know what that means, then I suggest you go look it the fuck up. But in the meantime, what you not gon' do is sit here— in a car I know my money paid for— and speak to me in no disrespectful tone. I don't give a fuck if it's Jesus or a nigga named James, ain't no man finna disrespect me. Period. As far as this little arrangement, nigga, it's a thousand Hotrod's out here. So let me know right now if I need to find a new one."

Because there was no profit in pride, and Mecca was his primary source of income, Hotrod knew it was best to put the petty emotion in his back pocket and sit on it. "Nah, you don't need to find nobody else," he meekly remarked. "And that's my fault if I offended you. Moving forward, I'll be more discreet when it's time to link up."

And that's how you put a nigga in his place, Mecca smiled to herself at how easily it was done.

As a gesture that all was forgiven, Mecca withdrew an envelope from her purse and passed it to Hotrod. "That's the other half."

The culprit responsible for injuring Asha, Hotrod's payment for the broad day attempt totaled twenty-five grand. And while Mecca had personally bore witness to the brazen attack, what neither of them suspected was that Asha survived it. Her death hadn't officially been declared by any news channels, but Mecca was assured by a source in Detroit that Asha was a brain-dead vegetable incapable of breathing on her own.

"You don't wanna count that?" Mecca asked Hotrod as he put the envelope in the center console without bothering to open it.

"I would if I didn't trust you."

She disagreed with his logic but held her tongue. After all, she was his employer, not his mentor. "So how soon you gon' slide on the other sister?" She asked in readiness for the hit on Noni to be handled. "I mean, they are twins. And since they came in this world together, I think it's only right that they leave it together."

As the two conspirators conspired on Noni's demise, Mecca's sister, Unique, stood in the front window of the beauty salon. Contrary to what Mecca was told, Unique knew for a fact that Asha had rumbled with the reaper and won. The girl was as close to a vegetable as an atheist was to God. But in Mecca's stubborn persistence to attain revenge, she couldn't see that her war had been waged with a much bigger force; for Unique truly believed that the twins were assisted by a guardian Angel. How else could you explain them appearing untouchable?

This girl out of control, she thought in concern over Mecca's behavior. *And I gotta do something before we both end up dead.*

Stepping back from the window as she scrolled through her Android, Unique tapped a thumb on the screen and brought the phone to her ear. When a hospital employee answered on the other end, Unique turned to retreat to her office for privacy. "Yes, ma'am, my name is Meridith Levan, with the felony probation department..."

Chapter 6

Asha was propped up in bed and watching TV when Noni appeared in the doorway of her room. As if nothing or no one existed in that moment, the siblings stare conveyed countless emotions— the most meaningful being the feeling of relief. Asha's little baby was safe, and Noni's mother-figure had survived five shots. While the love between them had already been boundless, the depth of it deepened from the close encounter with unbearable grief.

Asha was touched by the teardrops that trickled down Noni's cheeks. "Girl, if you don't get your little crybaby butt over her."

As if she hadn't just murdered two men in less than a week, Noni rushed into Asha's outstretched arms and bawled like a baby.

Placing kisses over Noni's hair while gently stroking it, Asha closed her eyes and silently offered her very first prayer. *Thank you for keeping us together, God. I know I don't know you like that, but I'm willing to try. I was once told you know the number of hairs on my head, so clearly you know the condition of my heart. I'm not a bad person and neither is my sister. So I ask that watch over us, and I'll talk to you later.*

Asha didn't know if it was all in her mind, but she felt a sense of serenity at the conclusion of her prayer. What if it had actually been heard by a Higher Being? Recalling the number of hurdles her and Noni overcame, the idea of there being a God wasn't too farfetched.

Once the tears were done flowing and their noses were blown, Noni sat on the edge of Asha's bed. "Look at you." She smirked, touching a hand to her bandaged head. "Out here in these streets like a Teflon don."

"I know, right?" Asha grinningly replied. "They must don't know real butterflies don't die."

Noni flashed a slight smile, then bowed her head and confessed, "I ain't gon' lie, twin, that was the worst fear I ever felt in my whole life. I don't think that's one I could've bounced back from. Because it's like..." she looked up at Asha, "you more than just my sister. You my heartbeat, and without you I'm dead. And I wanna say I'm sorry for anytime I ever made you mad. Asha, I love you more than I know how to explain, and I'll never take you for granted again."

"Awww," Asha crooned at her sister's heartfelt disclosure. "Listen at my lil' Noni being all sentimental. Come here and give mama some more of them hugs and kisses."

As they disengaged from a lengthy embrace, Asha held Noni's face in her hands. "I love you like I gave birth to you myself. So you more than just a sister to me, too. You my baby, and you'll always have your own section in my heart. But I want you to remember that loyalty is what defines us. So I don't want you feeling no type of way towards Shawna, as if this was somehow her fault. I had a choice to make in a split second, and I chose to be my sister's keeper."

Noni offered a solemn nod of understanding, and Asha lightened the mood with a knowing smile. "So tell me what my Noni been doing. Because I already know you been acting up."

Smiling at her mischief, Noni disclosed every deadly detail of her and Double-O's four-day purge. Then her voice grew quiet at the thought of young Teer, for she knew Asha would shoulder the blame of his untimely demise. So Noni decided she would tell her later.

When Noni noticed something had drawn Asha's attention, she turned just as Shawna was on the verge of knocking to announce her presence. "Hey, girl," Shawna nervously smiled as she entered the room, accompanied by Lo-Lo.

Noni immediately rose up from the bed. "Shawna, you can stay, but, Lo-Lo, you need to step."

"Are you serious?"

"As breast cancer," Noni coldly replied. "Now move your ass around."

"Noni," Shawna called, reaching to touch her arm in an effort to deescalate the situation.

"Watch out," Noni snatched her arm away from Shawna, then returned her attention to Lo-Lo. "You ain't welcome in this room, at least not while I'm here. My sister got shot in her muthafucking head, and *now* you wanna show up. Girl, if you don't get the fuck on."

"Noni, I've been stopping by for the last few days. And as soon as Shawna told me she was out of the coma, I came straight here."

"Aye, yo, you beating a dead horse." Noni ignored her claims. "This the second time some shit done happened and you showed *after* the fact. And all because you out running around with a nigga that probably got his hand in this shit."

"Noni, we was all the way in Chicago when it happened. So as much as you might not like him, he couldn't have had nothing to do with it."

Infuriated by Lo-Lo defending him, Noni clenched her fists and had to draw a deep breath to compose herself.

Lo-Lo stepped over to catch sight of Asha, but Noni moved over to obstruct her view. "She done did all the saving she gon' do for the month. So this my last time telling you..."

"Noni, I can't believe you coming at me like this," Lo-Lo shook her head.

"And I can't believe you letting some dick come between your loyalty to the Mob. After all we done did for your forgetful ass. After you swore you'd never put another man before your us again. But that's exactly what the fuck you done did. So I'ma need you stand on that shit."

Making his rounds, doctor O'Brien entered a room where the tension was thick as fog. After taking in Shawna's downcast expression, he turned to sternly address the room, "I'm sorry, ladies, but Ms. Kincaid needs to rest. As I'm sure you're aware, she sustained quite a few serious injuries. So maybe it would be best if you came back tomorrow."

"What about me, doc?" Shawna worriedly asked, hoping he wouldn't make her abandon her post.

"Well... I guess one visitor would be fine." He slipped her a wink. "But no more than that for now. I'm sure you can understand her recovery requires a great deal of rest."

As Noni hugged and kissed Asha before leaving the room, O'Brien regarded her with a curious eye. While he could tell from the intensity of her stare, she was capable of violence, he couldn't overlook the affectionate manner in which she embraced her sibling.

In the hospital's waiting room, Double-O stood up as Noni and Lo-Lo stepped in his direction. At a head gesture from Noni, he fell in line and trailed them to the elevator.

Once the three were on board and descending downwards, Noni glared at Lo-Lo, then addressed Double-O while staring straight ahead. "Aye, bro, why that nigga CJ take that trip for real?"

It took just a second for him to catch on. "Because he was plotting with the opps."

"Plotting on what?"

"To rob y'all."

"And who is these opps, bro? Or should I say, who *was* these opps?"

Double-O smirked. "That Bandgang nigga that got smoked on the bus."

When Lo-Lo looked up at hearing the victim's affiliation, Double-O added, "And that nigga Uno's first cousin."

A speechless Lo-Lo was grateful for the ding of the elevator as its door slid open. And if their claims were correct, Uno had a lot of explaining to do.

"Look at you," Noni scoffed at Lo-Lo in disgust as they exited the hospital. "You can't wait to run and confide in that nigga. But make sure you let him know, I'ma get to the bottom of it. And when I do, ain't nothing gon' stop me from upping the score."

No sooner than the threat left Noni's lips, time seemed to slow as she locked eyes with Uno— who sat behind the wheel of his candy Camaro. As badly as Noni wanted to give him the finger, she fought off the elementary urge and settled for a facetious wink.

Upon Lo-Lo lowering herself into the Camaro, Uno inquired, "Wassup with your peoples? She all winking at a nigga and shit."

Lo-Lo ignored his question to ask one of her own. "Why you ain't tell me that boy on the bus was your cousin?"

When Uno initially learned that the Greyhound victim was D-Nutty, he'd be a boldfaced liar if he claimed he hadn't felt more relief than grief— for he hoped the whole robbery idea would be buried along with him. But from Noni's wink to Lo-Lo's inquiry, Uno suspected the dilemma was far from over. And while authorities pled with the public for assistance in solving the daring murder, he had a pretty good idea of the blind man's identity and his ski-masked accomplice.

To Lo-Lo's question, Uno answered, "I didn't tell you because the nigga was on some different shit. I had to stop fucking with him. So I saw no point in even bringing him up."

"So it's true about him wanting to rob us?"

Uno confirmed the allegation with a subtle nod, and Lo-Lo exploded. "And you was just gon' let him? You wasn't gon' say shit to me? A heads up, or nothing?"

As Uno thought of how to best explain the position he was in, Lo-Lo eyed him with a sour look and slowly shook her head. "Maybe I was wrong about you. Maybe my peoples right, and you just think I'm some naive-ass white girl you can take advantage of."

Angered by the assault on his character, Uno leaned across her lap and opened the car door. "Get the fuck out."

"Excuse me?"

"I ain't stutter, you heard what the fuck I said. Get your hoodrat-ass the fuck out my car."

"Hoodrat?" Lo-Lo heatedly repeated. "Uno, you got me fucked up. Boy, don't play with me. I ain't no muthafucking hoodrat."

"Mannn." He waved her off. "Fuck outta here. Half the city done ran up in that lil' shit."

Enraged by the false accusations, Lo-Lo started swinging and screaming, "You got me fucked up, Uno! I ain't never been no hoodrat!"

Easily blocking majority of her blows, Uno grabbed her arms and began laughing; which only heightened her fury.

"Ain't shit funny," she wrestled to get loose.

"Nah, it really is, though." His expression turned serious. "Because look how you acting. Now you see how it feel to be called something you ain't. I'm just as much of a snake as you is a hoodrat. But if you gon' let people poison your mind, when you know who I am in your heart, ain't no way we can win. Because what chance do we got if we ain't got each other's back?"

When Uno released her, Lo-Lo sat back in the seat and considered his words with a thoughtful expression. Having to admit that he made perfect sense, this was one of the things she loved most about Uno— the way he could get her to see his perspective through fitting examples. Her man had the mindset of a boss, which was more appealing than the features of his face.

Easing the tension with a shameful chuckle, Lo-Lo turned to Uno and acknowledged his logic. "You right, bae, and I can't even argue with you. Because I was definitely heated at that hoodrat shit, and you had every right to get upset about what I said. I should've gave you time to explain before jumping to conclusions. So I'm woman enough to admit I was wrong."

After a moment of appearing to be thinking it over, Uno dryly replied, "Yeah, well... I guess I can accept your apology. Even though you didn't officially apologize, and say, 'Uno, I'm sorry, daddy, and it won't ever happen again. Now let me suck it and make it better'."

"Shut your nasty butt up!" Lo-Lo laughed, playfully nudging him. "And it usually take me a minute to admit when I'm wrong, so you should consider yourself lucky."

He grabbed his crotched and cockily grinned. "Nah, I don't think luck got nothing to do with it. You know you a addict for this dick."

Once the pair shared a laugh and a reconciling kiss, Uno slapped her thigh and told her to close the door. Lo-Lo crossed her arms in defiance. "I didn't open it. And I still feel some type of way about you telling me to get out. So if you really want me to stay, you know what to do."

Leaning over, like he intended to close it himself, Uno slipped his hand in her pants and caused her to gasp as he pinched her clit between two fingers. "Close that muthafucking door, before I make you bust a nut, right here in the open."

"Uno, stop," she whined, squirming from a touch that was more pleasurable than her own. "Stop before somebody see us."

"Then close it," he repeated, to which she clamped her thighs over his hand and reached to comply.

As he withdrew his hand with a triumphant grin, Lo-Lo shakily promised, "I'ma get you back. And when I do, I'ma make you beg for mercy."

His grin grew bigger at her pornographic pledge. "Bring it," he dared, then slowly sucked his fingers like he had dipped them in cake mix.

They were speeding through traffic, en route to his residence, when Uno inquired about Asha's condition. "So wassup with your peoples? Is she really out the coma?"

"Yeah, but I ain't even get a chance to talk to her. Shit went left soon as I stepped in the room."

There was a lapse of silence before he correctly presumed, "They think because dog was my cousin, I might be involved, huh?"

Lo-Lo slowly nodded, to which Uno reasoned, "Shit, I can't say I blame them, Lo'. They don't know me like that. And if roles was reversed, I'd be skeptical, too."

"What we gon' do, daddy?" Lo-Lo worriedly sought his advice. "It's like, ain't nothing I say gon' change their minds. And I know you ain't soft," Lo-Lo paused at the thought of Noni's subliminal threat, "but I don't wanna see nothing happen to you."

He reached over to clutch her hand in comfort. "For real, Lo', a muthafucka could talk 'til they turn blue in the face, and they still couldn't convince me you ain't my missing piece. And I'm saying, if the feeling is mutual, I think I might gotta plan. Because there's only one way we can make this work."

***

Back at Harper Hospital, Asha spoke to Shawna in a quiet but earnest voice. "...and that's why I said everything starts with a decision, love. So all you gotta do is make it, simple as that. It's just a matter of you facing your fears head-on."

"But is it really that simple?" Shawna implored. "Like, if somebody been doing something for years, or they've been stuck in a certain position for a real long time, is it really that easy for them to just up and change?"

"It is," Asha nodded in assurance. "And it's no different than an overweight person who dedicates themselves to dieting and exercise, or a woman who's been smoking cigarettes for years and quits cold turkey. You get fed up with your current situation, and you make a decision and stand on it. It's either you're in control of your mind, or your mind is in control of you. You can put it in your mind to do something and do it, or you can let your mind tell you you're not ready to do it. You just gotta decide which one is in control."

At Shawna's contemplative expression, Asha encouragingly continued, "It's time to spread them wings, love. You've been standing at the edge for long enough, and you gotta believe in yourself and just jump."

"But what if I can't fly, Asha? Then what?"

"But what if you *can*?" Asha countered. "And either way, you won't know 'til you try. So while I get started on this physical rehab, I'ma need you to get started on Big Baby's daycare."

"And what about the club? Who gon' take care of that?"

"Ray-Ray and Kiva can. If we can trust them with Polaris, then surely we can trust them with a club. And besides, they got way more experience than us, when it comes to running a club. I just need you to keep dropping the money off at the bank and let them handle the rest."

Asha hadn't failed to see how helpful Ray-Ray and Kiva became in the wake of Lo-Lo's absence. And their actions weren't meant to be a manipulative move; they were simply two women who noticed the opening of opportunity's window. A opportunist herself, Asha would reward their ambition with a management position.

Later that night as Asha lay in her bed, she thought about the contradictive counsel she'd given to Shawna. In a convincing tone she had told her best friend that everything begins with a simple decision. But Asha knew that if it was really that simple, she'd be able to get over her phobia of men. *I just wanna see my girl do good in life*, she thought in her defense.

Asha was dozing off when Shawna softly asked, "Asha, you sleep?"

"Not yet."

After seconds of silence Shawna sweetly announced, "I love you, Asha... even more than I do me."

Asha smiled in adoration of her adorable friend. "I love you, too, Shawna. You my lil' road dawg, for life. And you gon' be alright."

"But how you know, Asha?"

"Because I've never heard of an Angel that couldn't fly."

Chapter 7

Amid the city being dampened by a light round of rain, a Porsche Panamera skillfully weaved through afternoon traffic. Beyond its tinted windows, Double-O donned his hood as he handled the wheel. Beside him, Shawna focused on her lap and unconsciously toyed with her hands. And Noni was slouched in the backseat, caressing Martha with the brush of her thumb. Travelling in silence, the darkly clothed trio were en route to a dreadful event— Teer's funeral.

Upon Double-O slowing to a stop at a red light, a female pedestrian in possession of a purple umbrella proceeded to cross the street. When she peered at the Porsche while passing before it, Double-O felt his heartbeat quicken in response. Clocking her steps in a trance-like state, it wasn't until someone behind him honked their horn did he realize the light had changed.

As the sedan surged forward with a screech of its tires, Noni stared out her window at the woman with the umbrella, then observed Double-O with an inquisitive gaze. Despite being unable to establish the connection, she could tell that woman had deeply disturbed him. But because he didn't often speak of his past, Noni was clueless as to who she could be.

Minutes later Double-O turned into the parking lot of a Baptist church where he was met with an assemblage of adolescent males. Rocking powder-blue hoodies, they each had a portrait of Teer emblazoned on both sides.

With constant precaution as a standard requirement, Double-O and Noni wedged a weapon in their waistband before exiting the car. The streets were no longer being governed by codes, which meant drama could unfold while attending a funeral.

After greetings were exchanged between the two groups, Double-O led the way toward the building's front entrance. He appeared calm on the surface but was actually nervous, as he had always been fearful of a funeral service. Whenever he stepped up to a casket to pay his respects, he couldn't help but to wonder where he was on the list.

Stepping foot in the church, Double-O was sickened by the sight of the sizeable crowd. It was the fact that so few of these people were present when Teer had been barely surviving, but now chose to show up when it no longer counted. *This is a cold-ass world*, he thought. *They'll ignore you while you here, but come see you when you dead.*

As Double-O scanned the pews for a section that would seat the entirety of his group, he was approached by a gentleman whom he highly respected— Reverend Daniels.

Eyeing Double-O closely as the two shook hands, the Reverend leaned closer and quietly counselled, "Replace that fear with forgiveness, little brother. Without us granting to others, we can't expect to receive it from God. And due to certain lifestyles, some of us require more forgiveness than others."

Taken aback by the precision of the older man's counsel, Double-O regarded him with a reverent expression. How on earth had he known to address his fear of funerals? Or his anger at the attendants?

After directing Double-O to a section near the front of the church, Reverend Daniels took Noni aside to inquire about Asha. While explaining he'd stopped by Harper that morning and was told there was no such patient, he noticed that Noni wore one of the necklaces he had purchased for their 21st birthday.

Per Asha's instructions, Noni revealed that her twin was moved to a facility that specialized in physical therapy. "...the doctor tried to say she might walk with a limp, and we ain't hearing that. But she told me to tell you she finally had that conversation, and you would know what she meant."

The Reverend smiled, for he knew exactly what Asha meant. During their last encounter at the small diner, he encouraged her to have a conversation with God— and how she would rather it happen through prayer, then take place in person. "Send her my regards." He laid a fatherly hand on Noni's shoulder. "And tell her it'll soon be shown that she did the right thing."

As the crowd sat in silence once the service was set to begin, Reverend Daniels took his place at the podium and swept his gaze over everyone present. In his opinion, to radiate a virtuous energy was to establish a spiritual connection.

With the attendants undivided attention, and very little knowledge of the boy in the casket, Reverend Daniels delivered with passion a powerful eulogy. Aside from returning the young man's spirit to its Owner with a letter of recommendation, he encouraged the crowd to take advantage of life by adding value to themselves and those in their circles. "...as some of you may know, I wasn't always a Reverend, so I'll be the last to cast judgement if you've yet to take the step to connect with your Creator. However, I strongly advise you to cherish every second you spend on this earth. Because the reality is, you can check your bank account or wallet and know exactly how much money you got left. But there's nothing you can check to see how much time you got left. So spend it wisely. And remember, adding value doesn't necessarily have to be in monetary form. It can be something as simple as telling a friend you're proud of their progress and to keep pushing forward."

At the close of the eulogy Double-O rose, but remained in place as people formed a line to pay their final respects. His intention was to wait until the end and view the body in private. And as he remorsefully reflected on the short amount of time he'd spent with Teer over the past year, he was startled by the sudden uproar of a screaming woman.

"It should've been you in here, not my baby!" the woman wailed, aiming her finger and fury in Double-O's direction. "If they would've left your no-good-ass in jail, he'd still be here!"

Despite Double-O displaying no visible reaction, he recognized the face of a woman he hadn't saw in years— Teer's unfit mother. This was the woman who put her own child out in the cold because he couldn't get along with her boyfriend at the time. But on a planet where people preferred to avoid accountability, Double-O understood she had to blame someone for her parenting failures. So he crossed his arms and calmly absorbed the inaccurate accusations.

But as his calmness only caused her emotions to boil over, his infuriated aunt flew towards him. "You bastard!" She cursed him, assaulting his chest with the hammering of her fists. "It should've been you!"

As Double-O held up his arms to ward off the blows, his aunt was soon embraced by the woman with the purple umbrella. "It's gon' be OK, Fran," she buried her baby sister's head in her bosom and softly consoled. While continuing to comfort her sobbing sibling, the woman looked up at Double-O with the most tender expression.

Having noticed the woman's expression as they stood nearby, Shawna and Noni knew such a look of compassion couldn't come from a stranger.

If had been anyone other than his cousin in the casket, Double-O would've bypassed the viewing and made a beeline for the exit. He loathed attention and was so embarrassed. All the ogling eyes were a reminder of his childhood, when he was ridiculed in school over his jet-black skin and unattractive features. Oh, how he wished his aunt was a man, for he would physically ensure she regretted resurrecting those damaging memories.

Once the spectacle was over and only pallbearers were present, Double-O stood over Teer and took in his appearance. Appearing to be asleep, he wore his favorite Detroit Piston's jersey and a matching ball cap which was actually to cover his gunshot wounds. "Your story was way too short, lil' homie. And that's a regret I gotta carry 'til my turn come up. But I got that nigga, cuz. I know that won't bring you back, but in our world, revenge is all we got."

Double-O glanced over his shoulder before removing a weapon from his waistband. "I brought you something," he said to Teer, placing the pistol inside his casket. "This the one I used to put that nigga to sleep with. So may you rest well, my G."

Outside in the Porsche, with the drizzle now a downpour, Shawna and Noni were talking, when Double-O and others carried the casket from the church to a hearse. Sharing their opinions on Double-O's relation to the two women, the girls grew quiet as he returned to the car.

Soaking wet as he slid behind the wheel, Double-O sat there for a minute before voicing his decision to skip the burial. "And I don't wanna talk about it," he firmly added, then put the Porsche in drive and pulled out the lot.

Not far from the church, they all saw the woman with the purple umbrella as she stood at a bus stop. "Double-O, who is that?" Noni couldn't resist from asking, as she craned her neck to look through the rear windshield. When he failed to respond, Noni turned back around and roughly repeated, "Nigga, who is that?"

"My mama," he growled.

Shawna exclaimed, "What? Your mama? Man, we thought that was probably your sister. If you don't turn this car around and give your mama a ride." As he stubbornly continued to drive, Shawna sought Noni's assistance. "Noni, say something. We can't just leave that woman standing out here in the rain."

On account of the loveless relationship between her and her own mother, Noni was the wrong one to ask for help. "Shit, I ain't getting in that. That's between them two, I don't know their history. But clearly it ain't good."

Shawna wasn't having it. "Well, let me out, then."

Double-O glanced at her. "Let you out?"

"Yeah, you heard me. I'll find my own way home."

"Come on, Shawna, you can't be serious," Noni spoke up, as she could picture her sister's furious reaction if they abandoned Shawna on the side of the road.

"Oh, I'm serious as hell!" Shawna insisted. "My mama left me for dead, but I still wouldn't leave her standing out in no rain. Now, Double-O, I'm telling you, man, pull this stupid car over and let me out."

Also aware of how Asha would react, Double-O knew there was no way in hell could let Shawna out. So, though he hated the fact that his hand was being forced, he circled the block and braked by the bus stop.

Without closing her door, Shawna hopped out the car and approached the woman. Despite being unable to hear the exchange, Double-O's heartbeat pounded in nervous suspense. He hoped she'd decline the ride. It had been over five years since he last saw his mother, and he wasn't ready to face what would come with their reunion. This was the woman who had hurt him in inhuman ways. The woman whose relentless mistreatment molded him into a menace.

"I feel you, brodie," Noni said in sympathy as Shawna and the woman came toward the car. "But you know how Shawna is."

Upon Shawna opening the back door, the woman closed the umbrella and gave it a shake before entering the car. Tipping her head in greeting as she settled next to Noni, she peered up front at her son who stared straight ahead in refusal to acknowledge her.

Eager to dispose of his unsettling discomfort, Double-O sped off as soon as Shawna shut her door; with the rain slicked road causing the car to slightly fishtail before its tires caught traction.

At his mother's directions, they arrived at a west side shelter for women. Shawna regarded the residence with a curious frown. "Ma'am, this where you staying?"

She bobbed her head in humility. "I guess you can say I'm finally trying to get it together. You know they say, 'a fool at fifty is a fool for life', and girl, I'm almost forty-three."

It was during her preteen years when Double-O's mother, Maureen, fell victim to a crippling disease called low self-esteem. Without the supportive advice from a peer or a parent, she saw sex as a means to gain attention from men. While sharing herself with whoever showed interest, she had hoped that one would eventually take notice of the goodness in her heart. But as the ultimate result of her promiscuous ways, she'd been left with nothing but a necklace of regret that hung heavy around her neck.

After expressing her gratitude in regard to the ride, Maureen paused to look at her son with a thoughtful expression. "Marjuan, I know there's nothing I can say or do to erase the past but trust me when I tell you I'm paying for my mistakes."

When Maureen exited the car and gently closed the door, Shawna spun on Double-O with an eye of reproach. "You really just gon' let your mama leave without saying nothing to her?"

"You don't know what that woman did to me," he defensively replied.

"And you don't know what somebody did to her," Shawna sensibly countered. "In case you didn't know, *Marjuan*, hurt people hurt people. I ain't saying she wasn't wrong for whatever she did, but I'm saying you gotta give her credit for at least trying to be better. Because if it's impossible for a person to change, then I guess I'm still the same Shawna that was out here on drugs."

As Maureen stood on the porch and watched the Porsche pull off, her eyes bore a reflection of sadness from genuine remorse. Having given birth to Double-O at the age of sixteen, she had subjected him to torture that undoubtedly left him with untreated trauma. Submerged in shame that deprived of her sleep, she thought it was well deserved that her wake-up call had come in the form of an incurable disease known as HIV.

Chapter 8

Wearing workout gear and running shoes, the twins were in the exercise room of the rehab facility in which Asha had been admitted. In addition to her scheduled routines, Asha was initially convinced that additional work would accelerate her recovery. But, as Noni presently pushed her past her comfort level, Asha was becoming increasingly irritated with her instructor.

"Come on, twin, just give me ten more," Noni encouraged her as they faced each other and did leg lunges. "This how you gon' build your leg strength back up."

Asha wiped sweat from her forehead and complained, "How many more you want me to do, Noni? I've already did like a thousand."

"Girl, you ain't did nowhere near no thousand. So would you stop being lazy and start lunging?"

"I don't understand why you're trying to burn me out. You're taking all the fun out of it."

"Fun? This shit ain't meant to be fun. If that was the case, the whole world be in shape. Now quit all that crying and start bending them knees, I'm trying to help you."

"Yeah, well..." Asha picked up her towel as a sign she was done, "maybe I shouldn't have asked for your help, because you're clearly on some inconsiderate-ass shit right now."

"And you clearly on some ol', self-pity-ass shit right now," Noni called out as Asha walked off. "So gon' and limp your pitiful, weak-ass back to your room and lay down."

As intended, Noni's statement struck a nerve and caused Asha to pivot with fire in her eyes. "Ain't nothing weak about me."

"Shit, I can't tell. You running from a few lunges."

"I ain't running from nothing. I'm just in pain. I got shot five times, in case you forgot."

"Yeah, well, you should've thought about that before you got on your superhero-shit."

"I did that to save our little sister."

"But you can't do a lil' exercise to save yourself. It's funny how you'll go above and beyond for everybody else, but act like you can't do the same for Asha. So like I said, limp your pitiful, weak-ass back to your room and lay down."

"Noni, you ain't gon' keep disrespecting me."

"And what you gon' do about it, Asha? I wish you would try to hit me. I'll push your crippled-ass down."

As they pinned one another with an unblinking glare, Asha repeated her previous claim in a resolute tone, "Ain't nothing weak about me."

Noni just scoffed in response, to which Asha threw down her towel and, without breaking eye contact, began to do lunges. "Ain't nothing weak about me," she said at the completion of each repetition. And though the procedure was so painful that it brought her to tears, she exceeded the number of lunges her instructor requested.

Swelling with pride at her sister's perseverance, Noni's connection with her twin had her in tears as well. While it had hurt to address Asha in such a harsh manner, the rewarding result meant she had made the right move.

When Asha's right knee buckled beneath her weight, Noni was there to catch her before she could fall. As Asha broke down and sobbed into her sister's sweatshirt, Noni gently rocked her and whispered encouragement. "You did good, love. And everything gon' be OK. Because you Asha, my lil' Teflon don. And just like ain't nothing else been able to stop us, neither will this. We gon' get through it, I promise."

With one of Asha's arms draped around Noni to reduce pressure on her knee, they made their way back to Asha's private room where Noni ran her a bubble bath and helped her undress. Because it was Asha who always did the consoling, it made Noni feel good to reciprocate the treatment.

While tenderly bathing her as one would an infant, Noni observed the number of war wounds all over Asha's body. From the scars on her head to the one on her face, Noni was amazed at how something so beautiful could bear so many blemishes. *This girl a warrior for real*, she thought as she washed Asha's hair.

Asha's eyelids were closed as her scalp was massaged. "Thank you, twin," she softly stated.

"Aww, girl, this ain't nothing; all the times you've done it for me."

"Nah, I'm talking about you not letting me give up, earlier. I was being a baby, and you called me out. If I wanna bounce back, I'ma have to push myself super hard. Because Lord knows I ain't trying to walk with no limp."

Noni leaned down to kiss her cheek and assured, "Even if we gotta get it in three times a day, you gon' be good."

As the twins later exited the bathroom laughing at when Noni threatened to push Asha down, there was a knock at the door and they called out in unison, "Come in."

It was Ray-Ray and Kiva who entered the room, wearing classy attire and beaming smiles. "Hey, girl?" They exclaimed in excitement, taking turns to envelop Asha in a genuine embrace. What had initially begun as business had blossomed into a sisterly bond.

"Oh my God, look at you," Kiva complimented, as she held Asha at arm's length. "My girl done shook back like cooked crack!"

"And I know how you feel about the 'B' word," Ray-Ray chimed in, "but I swear you the most gangsterist bitch I ever met!"

Asha laughed. "I just know 'gangsterist' ain't nowhere in the dictionary."

"And I just know another Asha ain't nowhere in the city," Ray-Ray retuned. "You like *Lazarus*. They out here saying you got hit fifteen times. And when they see you up and walking, they gon' be bowing down to kiss your f —"

"Alright, Ray-Ray, we get it, got-damn," Kiva jokingly cut in. "And how this woman supposed to heal, if you got her head all swole up and shit?"

"Nah, watch out," Asha playfully swatted at Kiva. "Quit hating and let her finish, it was just getting good."

After they shared a laugh, Noni suggested that Asha should get off her knee and helped her in bed where she comfortably reclined against a number of pillows.

"But seriously though, Asha," Kiva said from the foot of the bed, "it's a relief to hear you laughing and shit. You really had a bitch worried to death. And I ain't just saying that on account of the position you've put me in, I'm saying because I mean it. Now, I'd be lying if I stood here and said I didn't love all the luxuries that come with my new lifestyle. Girl, you've done more for me in the last six months than anybody else done did for me since I been on this earth. And I'm saying, I'd hate to give it all back, but to help you get revenge on whoever did this, on my dead Nana, I'm willing to eat jail food for the rest of my life. You worth every ounce of loyalty I got, and that's pretty much all I can offer you in return. So let me know the next move, and I'm all in."

Her sincerity resonated with everyone present. But Ray-Ray was moved the most, for she knew her best friend was a disciple of distrust and slow to show emotion.

"I believe every word you just told me," Asha replied, returning Kiva's gaze with a fond expression. "And there ain't a doubt in my mind you willing to go the distance. But if you really wanna repay me, then just keep doing what you doing by standing on business. And whenever you get the chance, don't hesitate to help the next woman who worthy.

Because in case y'all forgot…" Asha looked at each girl. "We the brains behind this shit. A man just the body, but we the engine— which means it can't move without us. And I ain't saying every man ain't shit, but at the end of the day, it's us against them. Just think about it." Asha continued in a passionate tone, "Out of all the women going through domestic violence, who usually the ones abusing them? Out of all the women being raped, who you think doing the raping? Or when a woman get called out her name, because she don't wanna give up her phone number, who doing the disrespecting? And a lot of women don't know, but on the chess board, the Queen is the most powerful piece. Yeah, the King might be the most important, but the Queen is the most *powerful*; the one they depend on to protect that ass. But until we stick together and start demanding what we rightfully deserve, they gon' continue to downplay our value. And that's why I say help a woman in need every chance you get. Because we all we got."

While her spiel left them speechless, they had to acknowledge the validity of her views. The world was indeed imbalanced in relation to the rights of a woman. The woman whose womb was magical, and her wisdom was matchless. The woman whose resilience was remarkable, and her essence was angelic. The woman whose nurturing nature was what sustained life. And yet, the woman remained the most mistreated and unappreciated being on earth.

"Girl, you might be a prophet," Ray-Ray stated with a straight face. "Because I swear, I don't know no other woman thinking like you. Especially in Detroit. But everything you saying makes perfect sense. And not only that, but you actually make it possible to put people in position. So it ain't like you just preaching some shit. I can only imagine where you gon' be by the time you get our age."

"Wherever I am, I expect you to be there right with me." Asha smiled at both women. "Shit, the way y'all done stepped up, I gotta salute it. Taking care of Polaris, the club, just everything. Because regardless of what a person is offered, it's on them to do something with it. They say you can lead them to the water, but you can't make them drink. And I say, you can give them the game, but you can't make them think."

"Preach, got-damit!" Kiva leaned forward to high-five Asha. "On God, that's gospel."

As their conversation migrated to business related matters, Asha expressed her approval of the women's outward appearance. "I see y'all all dolled-up like barbies, too. I gotta say, you looking definitely looking the part of professional women."

"I mean, you know..." Ray-Ray grinned, brushing imaginary lint from her Tom Ford jacket, "as a manager of the littest club in the city, the status and the fabrics gotta match at all times."

"And I'm just saying," Kiva popped the collar of her Marc Jacobs blazer, "I'm trying to be a boss bitch's boss, you feel me?"

They were discussing an upcoming event that was being hosted at Skittles, when Asha cut Kiva off and inquired, "Aye, has Lo-Lo still been coming to the club?"

Ray-Ray and Kiva exchanged a look, to which Asha persisted, "Has she?"

With a shrug of her shoulders Kiva hesitantly answered, "I mean... she came through a few times."

"And what else, Kiva?" Asha prompted, sensing there was more to the story.

"Listen, I don't specialize in getting shit started or —"

"Kiva, what else?" Asha firmly repeated.

Kiva looked away and ratted on her girl. "One time, she came with that nigga, Uno."

"What?" Noni exploded. "She brought that bitch-ass nigga to the club? Twin, you hear this shit?"

Wearing a blank expression, Asha sensibly replied, "Getting all upset ain't gon' change anything but your blood pressure, love. At this point, it is what it is. Our job now is to just keep our vision clear of emotion and figure out the best way to move forward. Because you already know my motto: one missing monkey don't stop no whole act. The show must go on; simple as that."

Asha returned her attention to Ray-Ray and Kiva. "I want y'all to keep running up that bag. Don't let nothing interfere with business. As long as these niggas showing up and showing out, we ain't discriminating. Because a clown nigga's money spends just the same as the next. And far as Lo-Lo, that's still y'all girl, so don't change up the vibe on account of us. Now gone and get up out of here and get back to it. And remember what I said, 'the show must go on'."

Once the twins were alone Noni eagerly asked, "What you want me to do about Lo-Lo?"

Asha shook her head and simply answered, "Nothing."

"Nothing?" Noni scrunched up her face. "First, she brought this nigga to the hospital, and now she got him all up in the club. Come on, twin," Noni lifted her eyebrows for emphasis, "this some shit we need to address."

"And what you want me to do, Noni? Give you the greenlight to get Lo-Lo? Is that what you asking me?"

"Nah, I'm asking you to give me the greenlight to get all of 'em. And me and Double-O got chemistry, so we could put these dogs down in a weekend, I promise you."

Asha studied Noni closely. "And you could really get Lo-Lo, just like that? Without no remorse?"

Noni blinked before answering, "Look how she doing us, Asha. She turned on us. So every good deed she did up until this point don't matter no more. She betrayed us, love. She put another man before us, after she swore on her life she'd never do it again. We put our freedom on the line for that girl. Don't you know if we would've got knocked, they would've gave me a life sentence? So how she just gon' say fuck that type of loyalty and not expect me to be in my feelings?"

Asha took Noni's hand. "Even though I didn't pull the trigger, I know exactly how you feel. And I agree, what you did that night was the ultimate display of loyalty. You protected your sister by all means, which is not something a lot of women would've been able to do. And it's not that Lo-Lo forgot, or don't appreciate what you did for her. You gotta understand that this has nothing to do with the condition of her heart. Some women need a man's affection to feel complete, and Lo-Lo happens to fall in that category. Unfortunately for us, she fell in love with the wrong one again. But we can't move against our girl, because that's a scar I don't want on either of our conscious."

Chapter 9

"...and this is where the kitchen area will be," a female contractor pointed out to Shawna as they stood inside Big Baby's daycare. "And as you can see, there'll be plenty of room for staff and appliances. Oh, and someone should be coming out today to install all the G.C.I. outlets."

Holding Polaris by hand, Shawna smiled brighter than a child on Christmas. "It's all coming together so well," she approvingly stated to the brown skin contractor. "And I gotta say thank you, for being so patient with me. I know I be changing my mind about stuff, but this is my first time ever doing something like this."

"I promise, you haven't been a problem at all." She smiled at Shawna, lightly touching her forearm. "And it's not every day I come across a job this big, so believe me when I tell you the pleasure is mine. Now come on, I wanna show you where we'll put the play area."

Though the building was still in early renovation stages, it already bore a difference in appearance than it did when Shawna and Asha first stepped foot inside. In addition to being thoroughly cleaned with MRSA and bleach, walls had been erected to section off areas. If all went well and according to schedule, Big Baby's would open for business within the next three months.

As they were in the designated play area— where the woman explained how she planned to replace the light fixtures and lay down carpet, a barking puppy suddenly came running towards them.

"Oooh, a puppy!" Polaris exclaimed, pulling her hand free of Shawna's and bending to pet the grayish-colored animal.

The puzzled look on the contractor's face was identical to Shawna's who also had no idea of where the dog had come from. But her confusion was short lived, as Double-O and Noni soon appeared in the room.

"Wassup with the Mob?" Noni greeted Shawna and genuinely embraced her. Shortly after Asha's recovery, Noni sat Shawna down and apologized for blaming her for what happened that day. And of course, Shawna had forgave her and said she understood.

"Whose dog is that?" Shawna inquired, as they watched Polaris giggle with joy while it chased her around.

"It's hers," Noni answered, nudging her head at the child. "Me and Double-O just picked it up from the pound. They said she like two months old and her name Bella."

"Like, La Bella mafia," Shawna thought out loud, to which Noni affirmed, "Exactly. When they told me her name, you already know I wasn't leaving without her. And considering everything the little girl done went through, it was like, why not get her a companion? You know, something that'll play with her and protect her at the same time."

Polaris had once been attached to a certain teddy bear. But because the stuffed animal presumably brought back memories of her mother's murder, the little girl no longer had love for the bear. So, when purchasing the puppy, Noni hoped it would win the child's affection. And judging from the playful encounter she presently witnessed, it seemed to be love at first sight between Polaris and Bella.

After introducing the contractor to her friends, Shawna excused herself and took them aside to ask about Asha. "How is she doing? Did she ask about me?"

Noni looked at her crazy. "Girl, what type of question is that? You know damn well that women asked about you. Shit, she made me sit there and tell her every single thing about what you've been doing with the daycare. And she told me to tell you she love you, and to stay focused on fixing this place up, while she fix up herself."

While Shawna disapproved of Asha's decision to keep her at a distance, she knew her best friend had her best interests at heart. But what she didn't know was that Asha's decision would play a pivotal role in the ultimate outcome of Butterfly Mafia.

"Alright, girl, we gotta get on this road." Noni hugged Shawna goodbye. "We gotta go see a weasel about a snake. But if you need anything, dial my number before 9-1-1."

Noni waved at Polaris and smiled. "Bye, little girl. And have fun with your puppy."

With his mouth on mute during majority of the meeting, Double-O tipped his head at Shawna before following Noni outside to the car.

As they were on the verge of entering the Demon, which Double-O now had the privilege of driving, Noni eyed him over the hood and stated, "I should revoke your licenses, nigga."

He flashed a curious grin. "For what?"

"Nigga, I saw the way your lil' beady-ass eyes kept looking at my girl. What, you thought you was being slick?"

He averted his gaze in embarrassment. "Nah, it ain't even nothing like that."

"Yeah, that's what them lips say." She smiled, lowering herself into the car. "But them eyes say otherwise."

Double-O was turning on to the interstate when he solemnly stated, "Noni, you my girl, and I would never do nothing to betray you or rub you the wrong way."

"Come on, brodie, don't go getting all emotional on me. I already know where your heart at. And besides..." She shrugged in indifference. "I wouldn't even be mad if you tried to make your move. Y'all both been through some shit, so it might do more good than you think."

"Or it could backfire," he quietly countered.

"And why you think that?"

"I'm damaged goods, Noni. Besides being loyal to this street shit, I ain't really got nothing else to offer. I'm just a soldier, my baby. And I accept the reality that I'm probably gon' die alone."

Noni could only regard him with empathy, for her mind failed to come up with a suitable response to such a sad statement. This was an instance when Asha would've really come in handy.

Arriving in Flint, Michigan, they got off on an exit and headed to the residence of Polaris' grandmother, Ms. Eady.

"I hope this woman still around," Noni said as they slid through the impoverished community. "She might've smoked herself to death with that money we gave her."

They were nearing the two-story shack in which Ms. Eady lived when their attention was drawn to her front lawn— where her and a man were engaged in a heated exchange. He had his finger in her face, and his body language said he was seconds from striking her.

Knowing Noni was anxious to intervene, Double-O didn't even bother to properly park. It wasn't a secret she detested the sight of domestic violence.

"Eady, you gon' make me put my whole foot in your ass!" Her boyfriend barked within inches of her face.

"Nah, put it in mine!" Noni volunteered, as she hopped out the car and skipped toward the couple.

"And who the fuck is you?" He demanded, looking Noni up and down.

"A girl that hit back. Now raise your hand at me and see if I don't beat your coward-ass."

"Coward?"

"Them the only ones that hit women," Noni affirmed.

Just as the boyfriend announced he also hit men, Double-O rose up out the Demon, rocking his hood and a heartless expression.

When Double-O came around the car and stood beside Noni, the coward was not only concerned by the chilling intensity of Double-O's gaze, but the fact that his right hand was wedged within the pouch of his hoodie.

"All you gotta do is *blink*," Double-O told the coward in an unnerving calmness. "And I'll bury you right here in this front yard."

Swallowing the lump in his throat while careful not to blink, the coward retreated a step and wisely stood down. "Man, I don't know who y'all is or where y'all came from, but this between me and my old lady."

Noni shook her head. "Nah, not when you trying to put your hands on her, it ain't. That's when you put me in it. And my brodie on whatever I'm on. So I suggest you might wanna take a walk. And if she call me and tell me you hit her when we left... there's only one way I can make sure you won't do it again. Now step off, nigga."

With his eyes focused on the front pouch of Double-O's hoodie, he backpedaled to the sidewalk. Then, turning to jog across the street, he glanced over his shoulder and vanished between two vacant houses.

"Ms. Eady, you remember me?" Noni turned to the woman, who stared across the street with a troubled expression.

"Of course I remember you," she answered, bringing her yellowish eyes in alignment with Noni's. "Y'all got my grandbaby. But what I wanna is, what you made you run that man off like that? You done scared him half to death, now he might not never come back."

Noni frowned. "So you cool with him putting his hands on you?"

"Girl, look at me," Ms. Eady said in reference to her rough appearance. "I ain't exactly beating 'em off with a stick no mo'. And I don't know about you, but I don't like laying alone in my bed at night."

"Ms. Eady, I ain't here to judge you, I just thought I was doing the right thing. But maybe, you know," Noni withdrew a wad of blue bills from her pocket and brandished it, "maybe this can help make it right."

Ms. Eady's eyes enlarged in greed, then narrowed in suspicion. "Last time I had to give up my granddaughter. So what I gotta do this time?"

"I just need some info'," Noni plainly stated. "And whether it's helpful or not, the money still yours."

"Just some information?" the woman skeptically repeated. "That's all I gotta give you?"

Noni held up her right hand as a gesture of being truthful, and Ms. Eady inquired, "Alright, what you wanna know?"

"First, I wanna know if the name Mecca sound familiar to you."

Ms. Eady's reaction was an answer in itself as she nervously looked around like Mecca might be nearby. "What you wanna know about her?"

"Whatever you can think of."

Averting her gaze to eye the ground in deep thought, the woman weighed whether the risk was worth the reward. The payment for Polaris had long been gone, so she was certainly in need of what appeared to be a fortune. But what good would it do if she was not alive to spend it?

"I know you not from Flint, because I been here all my life," Ms. Eady looked up at Noni. "But if this conversation gets out, they'll be using that money to fund my own funeral."

Noni lowered her tone and wickedly assured, "I'ma put that green-eyed dog down myself. So the only way she can hurt you, is by haunting you in your dreams."

It was after Shawna disclosed Mecca's sighting just seconds before the shooting, when Asha realized it was the same woman she'd met inside the gas station. Mecca had complimented her hairstyle, all the while secretly knowing what was minutes away from happening. Noni was enraged by her bold audacity, but Asha calmly suggested that her and Double-O take a field trip to Flint. After Mecca had attended D'Aura's funeral, it was then they began to suspect she had ties to the city. And with Ms. Eady being a lifelong resident, she made the perfect person to bribe for information.

Following Ms. Eady inside her unkempt house, Noni and Double-O took a cringe-worthy seat on a sunken gray couch. As they were already literally itching to leave, they declined her offering of something to drink.

"I've been knowing Mecca a long time," Ms. Eady began, taking a seat on a adjacent couch. "Back when her and D'Aura went to the same school. And let me tell you, people knew back then she was gon' be a handful. Then once her daddy got killed, from that point on you were either family or for in her eyes. And she had these two crazy-ass cousins, Pee-Wee and Otha. The one had —"

"You said, Pee-Wee and Otha?" Noni interrupted, masking her surprise at hearing mention of the names.

"Mm, hmm," Ms. Eady confirmed. "Just as crazy as two road lizards. The one, Otha, went off and joined the army. But I heard he kicked out for doing some messed up stuff to them Muhammads over there."

Ms. Eady went on, but Noni no longer heard her as her thoughts had been captured by captions of the past. Pee-Wee was the monster who had sanctioned her rape, and Otha was the pervert who performed it. It had been less than a year ago, when she gunned them both down at Belle Isle Island. So to learn that the two men were related to Mecca, it now made sense why she sought revenge.

But Noni couldn't help but to wonder how the woman would respond if she knew the real reason behind her cousin's demise. Would she condone their barbaric behavior, simply because they were blood related? Or would she uphold the code to which all real women were morally bound?

"Excuse me, Ms. Eady, I don't mean to cut you off again," Noni interrupted her irrelevant spiel, "But what I really need to know is if Mecca still living here in Flint."

"I mean, you know, she gotta business or two right here in the city," she casually informed as if she knew more. "And her mama in a nursing home, so she can't go too far."

"And do you know the location of one of her businesses?"

Ms. Eady grinned like a Cheshire cat. "Now a piece of information like that might cost you a lil' extra."

Chapter 10

Parking his Camaro outside a recording studio, Uno leaned over to remove a Ruger P-95 from the glovebox. He checked to ensure a round was in its chamber, then de-cocked the weapon and wedged it at the small of his back. Unsure of what to expect— as his immediate presence had been summoned by the capo of his crew, he drew a deep breath and exited the car.

Inside the building, Uno encountered an unsettling scene that put him on edge. Wearing facial expressions as dark as their clothing, nearly every member of his Bandgang crew sat around in attendance. Some openly stared, a few lifted their heads, and others avoided his gaze.

"I'm glad you could make it," a voice said from behind, to which Uno quickly turned and saw it was Guru. With a blunt in one hand and a bottle in the opposite, his loose dreads framed his face in a sinister fashion.

"Damn, that's what we on?" Uno spoke over the incessant pounding of his heart. "Creeping up behind niggas and shit?"

"There's no need to be nervous unless you gotta guilty conscious."

"I ain't say shit about being nervous, and my conscious like water. But I'm saying, wassup? Because clearly you niggas ain't in here recording."

Guru sucked on the tip of his Backwood. "I got something I wanna ask you," he said, exhaling smoke from his nostrils. "And I need to look you in your eyes when I do."

Uno replaced a witty reply for a shrug of indifference. "A'ight, what's on your mind?

As if he had the power to perform a polygraph with his pupils, Guru eyed him closely and questioned, "Did you have something to do with that D-Nutty demo'?"

"What?" Uno scrunched up his face in disbelief. "That's what the fuck you called me here for? To ask me if I killed my own cousin? Nigga, what you sprinkle on that weed? Because ain't no way in hell you in your right state of mind... asking me no shit like that."

Guru sat down the bottle and passed the blunt. "Gang, you think I got some hoe in my blood?" He stepped up to Uno in a challenging manner.

Uno calmly shook his head. "Nah... and I know ain't none in mine."

While the two men engaged an intense staring match, Guru growled, "You either with us or against us, ain't no playing the fifty. So we wanna know." He splayed his arms. "Who side you on, Uno? Is you Bandgang, or Butterfly Mafia, nigga?"

Uno smiled. "I can't believe after all these years, you still questioning my character."

"And I can't believe you don't want no revenge. We just lost three of the homies, one of 'em being your own flesh and blood. And you ain't even *faking* like you wanna do something. So you saying a man should just overlook that? A man should just say, fuck how your actions looking right now?"

"And how my actions looking right now, 'Ru?"

"Suspicious, nigga. I know it was D-Nutty's idea to rob them hoes. And I also know you wasn't on it, that's why he brought it to me, to put pressure on your ass. Now all of a sudden that nigga end up dead. And what the fuck was he doing on a Greyhound, anyway? Seem like he had to be running from something."

"Bruh, I wasn't even in the city when it happened."

"Yeah, how convenient." Guru smirked as he reached for the blunt and returned it to his lips.

Shaking his head at the nonsense of Guru's claims, Uno looked around the room. "Y'all really think I had D-Nutty lined up? My own family?"

"It don't matter what they think," Guru spoke up. "It's about what I know. And I know for a fact two people pulled down on D-Nutty girl right before he got kilt. And just so happen..." he paused to hit for dramatic purposes, "one of them was a light skin bitch with a butterfly tatted on her face. That picture ring any bells, nigga?"

Every felon in Detroit either knew or had heard about the twins with the blue butterfly on their cheek. Whenever their names were mentioned, it was the first description given to establish identity. So with Guru offering evidence of their likely involvement in D-Nutty's death, Uno knew he had just been backed into a corner— with the only way out by proving his allegiance.

"So here's the deal," Guru continued, giving Uno no options. "You gon' mash the gas on that white bitch. Make her tell you everything about anything, especially where they hiding that cheese at. And with the main one out the picture right now, them hoes vulnerable. So we can wipe them down from the inside out."

Using Guru's assumption that Asha was dead to his advantage, Uno attempted to discourage him. "Bro, and that's another reason why we should put this move on hold. Because since that shit happened, they ain't even been doing shit. They shut down their buildings and everything."

Not easily deterred, Guru returned, "Nigga, you don't think they already gotta million in a safe somewhere? And all you gotta do is find out where it's at. But if I'm asking you to do too much, then bring that white bitch to me and I'll handle the rest." Despite Uno declaring he'd get on top of it, Guru could sense his inner turmoil and openly told him, "My nose wide open, so them hoes getting it regardless. But I'm saying, I'd rather share it with you, than divide it without you. I got love for you, Uno, and I'd hate to see us end up on opposite sides. So tell me right now," he held out is hand for his comrade to shake, "is you Bandgang, or not?"

While Uno entertained the idea of drawing the Ruger and gunning Guru down, he wisely dismissed it as a suicidal move; for majority of the room were his loyal supporters. So he put on his most sincerest expression, looked Guru in the eyes, and lied without blinking. "I'm Bandgang Uno 'til my casket drop."

Giving no indication he detected the dishonesty in Uno's pledge, Guru embraced him. "Tighten up, my baby," he spoke in Uno's ear. "Don't ever let a bitch come before the Gang... shit like that can be bad for your health."

When the two disengaged, Guru's eyes held a strange look, then nudged his head and smiled. "Come on, I want you to hear this new shit I just wrote."

The Bandgang group had an upcoming show and were projected to perform in front of a sold-out crowd. With Uno being their most talented artist, he was expected to edit and enhance the quality of their music. Aware of their need for his artistic ability, he would buy himself time by revising their verses. Then, immediately after the show, he'd pocket his percentage and set his plan in motion.

It was near 1A.M. when the Bandgang clan began filing out the studio. Watchful of danger that often lurked in darkness, several of the men wielded weapons impregnated with hundred-round drums.

After ensuring Guru and his gang would resume their revisions the following day, Uno tucked himself in the Camaro and sighed in relief. He'd been inside that studio a total of four hours, wondering every minute if his life would be ended by someone from behind.

As Uno pulled out the parking lot, he drove past Guru and saw him doing something in the trunk of his car. When Guru sensed someone staring and looked back to see Uno, he flashed a smile and slammed the trunk closed— but not before Uno had noticed the enclosure was covered in plastic.

What Uno didn't know was that if he hadn't pledged his allegiance to Bandgang or had appeared to be dishonest, the plastic-wrapped trunk is what Guru had planned to haul his dead body in.

***

Upon Uno returning home to his apartment, he stood in the doorway of his room and beheld Lo-Lo as she laid facedown across his king-size bed. With her creamy skin clad in a sheer nightgown, his gaze lingered on the cuff of her voluptuous cheeks.

"Knock, knock," Uno tapped on the door, to which Lo-Lo looked back with tear-stained eyes. As caution caused him to immediately reached toward the small of his back, he lifted his head at Lo-Lo in a gesture that was meant to inquire if a sinister presence awaited him in the room.

Initially confused by the weapon and his tense expression, Lo-Lo soon made the connection and calmed his concern. "No, it's nothing like that, Uno, you're good. I just got a lot on my mind, and I'm emotional right now."

Exhaling in relief for the second time that night, he laid his gun on the dresser and joined Lo-Lo on the bed. "What's wrong, Lo'?" He rubbed her hair in a comforting manner.

"Everything," she mumbled, turning away to lay her face on the back of her clasped hands.

"What you mean?"

Lo-Lo didn't answer; her silence signifying she wasn't ready to discuss it.

Wise enough not to press her, Uno leaned down and touched his lips to her hair. "We gon' be good, Lo', I promise," he whispered in her ear. "As soon as I do this show, I'ma put the bread from that with what I already got and we getting on that road. I was waiting to tell you, but I found us a nice lil' spot down in Houston."

When Uno had previously mentioned that there was only one way for their relationship to work, the plan he proposed to pack up their most valuable possessions and move out the state. With her girls against him and his crew against her, he assured her there was simply no other alternative. "But what about my brother?" She had asked to which Uno explained that he could parole to their new house. Observing the reflection of sincerity in Uno's eyes, Lo-Lo had agreed to go with him.

"We gotta bright future ahead, and all we gotta do is get there," Uno continued, grazing his hand along the curve of her spine. "But for right now I just want you to relax, while I take you somewhere that'll make you feel better."

Removing his shirt, Uno got behind Lo-Lo and lifted her gown to expose a symmetrical bottom that still left him spellbound. After a moment of admiring its proportionate plumpness, he pried the cheeks open and dove face-first into her vaginal pool. But in his carrying out the unselfish act in accordance with her mood, he tenderly suckled the vulva and clit at a turtle-slow pace.

Despite the pleasurable talents of his certified tongue, Lo-Lo was unable to fully enjoy it. As a steady stream of tears slid from the corners of her eyes, she bit back a sob and suffered in silence. While her love for Uno was undeniably strong, the overweight guilt she felt for forsaking her friends weighed heavily on her soul.

Chapter 11

Alone in her room at the rehab facility, Asha wore a grimace of pain as she performed a set of explosive lunges. She was not only determined to bounce back completely, but to come out stronger than she was when the incident happened.

"I'ma warrior!" She emboldened herself while pushing through the pain.

Toweling the sweat from her face at the completion of her workout— which consisted of lunges, squats, and shoulder routines with lightweight dumbbells, Asha went into the bathroom and cut on the shower. After adjusting the water to a near scalding degree, she began peeling off her sweat-soaked clothing. Once fully undressed, she stood motionless for a minute, then gradually moved toward a full-length mirror.

For the first time since the shooting, Asha took in the reflection of her latest war wounds. Skipping past the scar beneath the butterfly on her cheek, she slowly traced a finger over the scar along her neck, which luckily for her larynx had only been a graze wound. She turned to inspect the dime-sized wounds on either side of her shoulder; fortunate that the ligaments didn't suffer permanent damage. Unable to get a good look at her back, she bowed her head and felt where the bullet had entered and exited, grateful it hadn't exploded into fragments. She'd been told that the hair in those two areas would never grow back, but something so trivial was the least of her worries.

"Damn, little girl, you done been through some shit," she told her reflection in the mirror. "And I guarantee it's nowhere near over."

After taking a nice, long shower— where she was able to gather her thoughts, Asha had thrown on something comfortable and now relaxed in her bed. She considered calling Shawna but decided against it, for the girl had to learn to be more self-sufficient. And besides, they had just talked last night, exchanging hours of encouragement on one another's progress.

Asha flicked through the channels for something to watch, when her search was cut short by a knock at the door.

"Come in," she permitted, assuming it was a nurse doing their hourly rounds. But the visitor that entered was not who she expected.

"Wassup with that Mob life?" Lo-Lo greeted with a nervous smile.

Masking her surprise with a neutral expression, Asha cordially replied, "Wassup wit' it?"

Not knowing whether or not if she should close the door, Lo-Lo just pushed it up, took a deep breath and turned back to face her childhood friend. "Listen, I understand if you don't want me here, but I just had to come tell you, I miss you, Asha. I miss all y'all. And I still love you as much as I have ever since we been friends."

"I hear you, Lo', but your actions ain't matching your words right now."

Lo-Lo opened her mouth to speak but Asha beat her to it. "You went against the Mob, girl. And you know I'm not the type to throw shit up in your face, but we've went above and beyond to prove our loyalty to you. You really hurt us, Loretta, and that's just me being honest."

"I know, and I'm sorry, Asha." Lo-Lo moved closer to the bed. "But I need you to understand that I've never in my life felt this way about a man. You know I would never do anything to hurt or betray you. I look at you like my sister. And if roles were reversed, I promise I'd be more understanding of your feelings. So why can't you do the same for me? Why can't you understand I'm in love, Asha? I'm not asking you to relate, I'm just asking you to understand."

Unmoved by her spiel, Asha replied, "I do understand. It's you who don't. But regardless of the next woman's outlook on friendship, I know what it means to be loyal to loyalty. I'm willing to die or do time for either one of mines, and you of all people should know that about me. But it's like you forgot our creed: By L.O.V.E. We Abide. And far as me being understanding about you being in love, I told you I'd never interfere with whatever made you happy. But when you playing with fire that will likely burn us all, then I gotta intervene. The well-being of my sisters will always come first. Because nine times out of ten, everything else is just temporary. But BFM is for life!"

"I hear what you saying, and I don't disagree with none of it." Lo-Lo reached out to take Asha's hand. "And the last thing I want you to see me as is a disloyal person. But, Asha, if you would please just do me one favor. Just have a conversation with Uno. Just give him a chance to explain the position he's in. Because how can you judge him, if you don't even know him?"

Asha sadly shook her head at her best friend's failure to see the full picture. "I've literally said everything I can to get you to see it, Lo', but you're so blinded by love that you won't even open your eyes. And I've never accused him of being a bad person. For all I know, his hands could be clean. But I don't need a conversation to tell me what I already know. And what I know is that his peoples robbed and killed Lil' Teer."

"But he didn't have nothing to do with that. Asha, he didn't even rock with his cousin like that."

"At this point it don't even matter," Asha reasoned. "Because they got their sights set on us now. So it's just a matter of time before they jump out there again. And if you thinking that boy can stop it from happening, you're next in line for a shrewd awakening."

"So what difference would it make if I left him alone, then?"

"Because then we could protect you from what's bound to happen. But let me ask you something. What did you hope to accomplish by coming here to see me? Be honest."

"Asha, I miss you so much, that I've been literally crying myself to sleep at night. I can't imagine us not being friends. But it's like, I also can't imagine not having Uno as my partner. He so good to me, Asha. He funny as hell, and I know you'd like him if you had a chance to know him. But me being honest like you asked, I guess I was hoping you would make an exception and accept my feelings."

"What if I accept your feelings and something go wrong? What if I accept your feelings and something happens to my twin? Or Shawna? Do you know there'd be no amount of crying or apologizing you could do to make that right? I'm sorry, Lo'." Asha shook her head in firm refusal, "But that's a risk that will never be worth taking. And I hate to make it seem like I'm turning my back, but you turned yours first. You put a man before the Mob, and that's just something my loyalty won't allow me to accept."

Saddened by the finality in her friend's tone of voice, Lo-Lo teared up. "Asha, what I'm supposed to do without you, girl? We've been friends forever."

As much as it pained her to do, Asha withdrew her hand from Lo-Lo's and turned her head in the opposite direction; a gesture that signaled their conversation was over. Lo-Lo had made her decision, and now Asha made hers.

With her head down as she moved from the bed, Lo-Lo got to the door and paused. She looked back, hoping for Asha to make eye contact. But after a wishful moment, she realized it wouldn't happen and sadly departed.

The second Asha heard Lo-Lo close the door on their friendship, she buried her face in the pillow to smother her sobs. Severing ties with Lo-Lo was the most difficult decision she had ever had to make. But because loyalty was the virtue Asha valued the most, she had to firmly ensure that everyone in her circle lived by the same standard.

After crying till her tear ducts were empty, Asha went into the bathroom and blew her nose. As she stood at the sink, lost in deep thought, she wondered if Lo-Lo would return to her senses before it was too late.

When Asha lifted her head, she was startled by the mirror's reflection of a presence behind her. "Who the hell is you?" She whirled toward the intruder, certain she wasn't an employee of the facility. "And what you doing in my room?"

Removing a pair of Aviator shades, the intruder replied, "My name Unique, and I'm here to get answers."

Unique? Asha thought, then recalled Double-O once disclosing that that was the name of Mecca's sister. But in knowing the snake could've already struck— had that been its intention, Asha kept her cool and calmly inquired. "Answers on what?"

"My cousins, Pee-Wee and Otha."

Though the names resurrected bitter memories of the past, Asha shook her head and lied. "Never heard of them."

"I think you have," Unique insisted, reaching back to shut the bathroom door. "In fact, I know it."

As Asha planted her feet in preparation for battle, Unique took in her stance with a smirk of amusement. "Girl, you know you ain't in no shape to be fighting. And like I said, I'm just here to get answers."

"And what if I ain't got them?" Asha stubbornly replied.

Unique began undoing the buttons of her jacket. "Then, may the best woman win."

***

Wearing headgear and boxing gloves, Noni was inside the ring at her gym. Actively engaged in an unusual sparring match, her coach had her boxing against two skilled opponents of the opposite sex. He didn't possibly expect her to beat both boys, but to simply keep up— which would sharpen her skill on every spectrum of the sport. His opinion was that if his fighter could make it through multiple rounds with two talented males, then surely she'd have an advantage over the average female contender.

Coach Bell blew his whistle and called Noni over to the corner of the ring. "You doing good on defense, but you're looking lazy," he quietly counseled. "So I wanna see a bigger output. That's how you get gas in that reserve tank. So when others get tired, you just getting started."

"Yeah, but it's boring as hell in this empty-ass gym," Noni complained as he removed her mouthpiece. "It's hard to get live, when ain't nobody looking."

While coach Bell understood she thrived on attention, there was a reason he declined to have spectators present. "Noni, trust me, I know you do better in front of a crowd. But I guarantee ain't no other girl in the game sparring with two boys at the same time. So this like our cheat code to the top. The way you gon' be running through shit, they gon' have to take notice. And you do want a shot at the title, right?"

She nodded, to which coach Bell advised, "Then, we gotta keep this on the low. Because the last thing we need is others knowing or doing what we doing. And if we gotta bunch of people standing around, that's exactly what'll happen. Now, let me see you do better on offense."

As he reinserted her mouthpiece and she returned to the center of the ring, coach Bell summoned the presence of her two sparring partners. "I ain't even gotta tell y'all how I feel about this fighter," he warned the two boys who also boxed at his gym. "But I want you to get a little more aggressive. She got the potential to put the spotlight in this place, and it's on us to make sure it happens. So, let's make her work."

In spite of Noni only having a few amateur fights over the course of her career, Coach Bell had her registered with the boxing as a professional fighter. The girl was naturally gifted, with skills it took others years to acquire. So, because he wholeheartedly believed she was capable of competing with the current contenders in the women's division. He felt confident about her upcoming debut fight at the Huntington Center in Toledo, Ohio. With the match scheduled to take place in front of 4,000 people, it would serve as the co-main event to Toledo's own rising heavyweight star, Jared 'Big Baby' Anderson.

Coach Bell watched in approval as an outmatched Noni held her own in the ring. She would deliver a lightning-fast combo to the head or body of one opponent, weave most of the shots from the second, then use her footwork to flee from being trapped in a corner. Never in his life had he witnessed a woman with such exceptional talent.

Noni suddenly dropped her guard and ate a crushing right hook that sat her on the canvas. As coach Bell climbed through the ropes in alarm, Noni shook off the daze and returned to her feet. "Noni, what the hell was that?" he asked in concern as he came to her aid. "Why you drop your hands like that?"

She spit out her mouthpiece. "Pull my gloves off, coach. I gotta go."

"You gotta go? Go where?"

"I gotta go check on my sister. Something ain't right, I can feel it."

He laid a hand on her shoulder. "Noni, this fight gon' be here before you know it. I thought this was what you wanted?"

"It is what I want, but my sister what I need. I just gotta go check on her real quick, and I'll be right back."

Once her gloves were removed, Noni climbed out the ring and ran to her locker room. Retrieving her phone from her Jordan gym bag, the first thing she saw was the missed call from Asha. As she returned the call in a mild state of panic, she pleaded with Asha to pick up her phone. Cursing at the sound of her sister's voicemail, she disconnected the call and dialed her again. When Asha failed to pick up after the fourth attempt, Noni sent Double-O a 9-1-1 text. Come get me!!!

Chapter 12

Shawna bore a beaming smile as she exited the prison where Kavoni was housed. Unlike last time, their visit ended on a more pleasant note— mainly due to her delivering good news. His appeal lawyer had found a loophole in his case and would be requesting the courts to grant a new trial. After serving over five years for crimes he didn't commit, Kavoni McClain could possibly be awarded a second chance at life.

From behind the wheel of the Porsche Panamera, Double-O observed Shawna as she returned to the car. He could tell she was excited, and it warmed his insides with unfamiliar sensations. Having never been in love, or even a regular relationship, it frightened him to feel a sense of attachment to the opposite sex. But Shawna owned an angel-like innocence that impelled him to protect her from the harms of this world.

Reentering the car, Shawna practically plopped on the passenger seat in pure joy. After peering over her shoulder to check on Polaris— who held Bella in her arms, Shawna turned back to Double-O and rattled off every detail of her visit with Kavoni. In her bubble of excitement, she was unaware of the nonstop pace at which her words poured out.

Double-O pulled off and just patiently listened, retaining what he could and nodding his head on occasion. And besides, Kavoni would soon reach out for an unrecorded conference.

As Shawna continued to ramble while they rode down the interstate, Polaris interrupted with a hopeful request. "Shawna, can we go to McDonald's?"

Shawna closed her eyes and groaned in euphoria, for the little girl's request was like music to her ears. While it wasn't a mystery McDonald's was her favorite, Polaris hadn't personally requested it since the death of her mother. So to hear her actually ask for it herself meant she was making improvement; and Shawna was certain it was courtesy of the pitbull puppy Noni had purchased.

Turning in her seat to lay eyes on the adorable 5-year-old, Shawna granted her request with the most loving expression. "Of course we can, sweetie. We'll stop at the next one we see, okay?"

Polaris nodded, then took advantage of Shawna with her big brown eyes. "And can Bella have some, too? I've been telling her how good it is."

"And Bella can have some, too," Shawna readily consented. What Polaris didn't know was that if she had asked for the world, Shawna would've figured out a way to make it hers.

"Did you hear that, Bella?" Polaris said to the puppy, whose response was to lick on the little girl's face. "We going to McDonald's to get some chicken nuggets."

True to her word, Shawna got Polaris' attention and pointed out a sign that showed a nearby McDonald's.

After ordering their food through the drive thru, Double-O backed into a parking space and Shawna passed a bag of nuggets over the seat to Polaris.

"Bella, wait!" Polaris giggled, as the dog was determined to stick her head in the bag. "I gotta get them out for you."

Adjusting the rearview mirror so she could watch their humorous interaction, Shawna would never admit she was a tad bit jealous of the inseparable bond between Polaris and the puppy. She knew it was selfish— considering how the animal proved to be therapeutic, but she had loved the idea of having the cutest little 5-year-old all to herself.

As if Polaris sensed Shawna's sadness, she looked up and caught her eyes in the mirror. In the sweetest gesture only a child could accomplish, she melted Shawna's heart with a wave of her chubby little hand.

They were back on the road and several miles from Detroit, when Double-O got the text from Noni. Upon noticing it was written in all caps, he called her.

"Bro, where you at?" She answered after only one ring.

"I'm right outside the city," he casually replied through his left Air Pod.

"You still with Shawna?"

"You already know."

Noni cursed. "Alright, well, drop her off and meet me at the rehab. Asha ain't answering, and something ain't right."

"And what you about to do?"

"I'm about to call an Uber, nigga. I ain't got time to be waiting on your ass. So drop her off and meet me out there."

Before Double-O had the chance to tell her he could be at the gym in under ten minutes, Noni ended the call.

"Who was that?" Shawna inquired.

"Who was what?" He dumbly replied.

"Double-O, don't play with me. Who was that?"

"I'm saying, you don't think that's a little nosey?"

"Not when it's about one of my girls, it ain't. Now is you gon' answer my question, or do I need to pull out my phone and make some calls myself?"

"I mean, you can if you want." Double-O shrugged. "But ain't nothing going on. And if it was, I would personally make sure you was the first to know."

Double-O had never been happier to see Big Baby's daycare, than when he turned into its parking lot. And luckily the building's renovation was currently underway. "Listen, I ain't trying to be rude, but I got something I need to go handle real quick. But just call me when you ready, and I'ma come pick y'all back up."

After Asha decided it was best to keep Shawna at a distance from their dangerous lifestyles, she got her a nice little two-bedroom apartment on the outskirts of the city.

"Double-O, I'm telling you, man. If something wrong with one of my girls and you ain't telling me... Oooh," Shawna shook her head as if to suggest there would be severe consequences.

While he wanted to smile at the cuteness of her unspoken threat, Double-O kept a straight face and reassured Shawna, "If something was wrong, you'd be the first to know."

Shawna wasn't convinced, which was why she exited the car without a word in return. "Come on, Polaris," she called to the child upon opening the back door. "Let's go check on Big Baby's."

Despite Shawna closing the door with more force than was necessary, Double-O still waited until they were safely inside before pulling off.

As he sped down the highway, Double-O shook his head and smirked. In spite of having limited knowledge on the opposite sex, what he did know was that a woman's intuition was usually on point.

***

"What!? Are you serious?" Noni exclaimed, as Asha recited her bathroom encounter.

"Girl, I was just as shocked as you."

There was a knock at the door, followed by Double-O announcing his presence.

Checking the peephole before unlocking the door, Noni pulled him in the room by the sleeve of his hoodie. "Bro, you ain't gon' believe who Asha had in her room," she said, closing the door and relocking it.

"Who?"

"Unique."

"Unique?" He disbelievingly repeated, to which Asha nodded from where she sat on the bed.

"Yeah, bro, Unique. That girl, Mecca, sister. I don't know how she got in here, but she did."

As Double-O's mind was flooded with puzzling questions, there was one in particular that greatly concerned him. "How she know where you at?"

Equally baffled, Asha shook her head. "I don't know, and she ain't say. Like I told Noni, I was in the bathroom at the sink, I looked up at the mirror and she was standing behind me. Talking about she want answers."

"Answers about what?" Noni and Double-O asked at nearly the same time.

Asha looked at her twin. "About them dudes, Pee-Wee and Otha."

Double-O frowned, for he knew the two dead men were related to Mecca. "Y'all knew them niggas?"

Because Double-O was now someone they trusted, Asha revealed, "They the ones that killed our mama in that home invasion."

As he recalled the footage of the double murders at Belle Isle, Double-O didn't have to be told that Asha and Noni were the two killers in the video. With the pieces coming together to form a complete picture, he now knew the reason behind Mecca's revengeful obsession with the twins.

"So, what you tell her?" Noni asked her sister, curious to hear how she handled the situation.

Asha's answer was simple, but took Noni by surprise, "I told her the truth."

When Unique had closed the bathroom door and removed her jacket, she wasn't preparing for a fight, but was in the process of undressing to show Asha she wasn't wearing a wire. Once she stood stark naked, she lifted her arms and turned in a circle. "It's just you and me," she'd then told Asha. "Woman to woman. And all I wanna know is what did they do to make y'all do what y'all did. Because my intuition telling me it was something really foul."

Relying on pure instinct, Asha had decided the woman was worthy of being told the truth— which was what she did with a direct stare. "When I was sixteen, they killed my mama and raped my twin. I had to watch that grown-ass man violate my lil' baby. So if you expect me to feel remorse for what happened to them, I don't. I won't. They got what they deserved for what they did to my twin. And if the shoe was on the other foot, I'd expect you to feel the same."

Upon Noni hearing that her secret had been shared with a stranger, she studied the floor. Not even Lo-Lo had known about the sexual assault. And while she initially wanted to be angry at Asha, she knew that her sister rarely made the wrong move. But more importantly, she Asha loved her more than anything in the world. So she'd respect her judgement, and trust that her decision had been based on wisdom.

Not one to miss a beat, Double-O felt the temperature change in the room. Whatever *the truth* was that Asha spoke on, he could see it was something that affected Noni's energy. But being a man who believed in minding his business, he kept his lips pressed together and his eyes on the ceiling.

As Asha took in her sister, she understood Noni had a right to be upset. She was ashamed of the experience, and wanted less people to know about it as possible. And although she felt bad for exposing her secret, Asha believed in her heart she had made the right call. Because had she not been honest, who knows how that bathroom encounter could've ended. But nevertheless, it bothered her deeply to hurt her Noni's feelings. *I'm sorry, twin,* she silently apologized, to which Noni looked up and the two locked eyes. Through an unspoken language only they understood, Noni told her sister she forgave her and accepted her apology.

"So what she do after you told her that?" Noni then asked Asha aloud, referring to Unique's reaction upon learning of the rape.

Asha flashed her famous mischievous grin. "She gave me her blessings."

There hadn't been any doubt in Unique's mind that Asha was being truthful about what had happened. And to hear that her cousin was a child molester made her sick to her stomach. Family or not, a sexual predator was deserving of death.

"I can't change what my peoples did," Unique had said as she began getting dressed. "And as a standup woman, I don't agree with their actions at all. Shit like that ain't never supposed to happen, whether it's to a child or adult. Regardless of how deep a person is in the streets, there's certain boundaries you just don't overstep. Like, harming an innocent woman, for one. So you might wanna holler at these two lil' niggas name Hotrod and Dogbite. And you know, they love them strip clubs in Flint. And don't be surprised to find out that D'Aura's blood is not the only blood on their hands."

After saying how Unique had gave her blessings, Asha felt like the kid with a secret as she witnessed the eager expression her sister reflected. Even Double-O had lowered his gaze from the ceiling to regard her in curiosity. They wanted to know what blessings Unique could've possibly given.

"Well, basically..." Asha only offered a hint to heighten the suspense. "She gave me a means to an end."

Noni shrugged in irritation. "Alright, and what's that? I mean, clearly I wasn't there. So stop acting like a kid and spit that shit out."

"Damn, Noni, why you always gotta ruin my lil' moments?"

"Moments? How the fuck you think this a moment, when that woman could've hurt you, or anything?"

"But she didn't."

"But she could've."

Double-O loudly sighed before cutting into their quarrel. "Are y'all really about to be arguing at a time like this? And you know I never pick sides, but, Asha, you can't be mad at your sister for being concerned. That outweighs whatever moment you thought you were having. Now will you please tell us what that woman said?"

Asha crossed her arms and reluctantly answered. "She told me who killed D'Aura, and who shot me at the gas station."

"What?" Noni exploded, as she flew to her feet. "Are you serious?"

Asha nodded, and Noni went over to cradle her head against her stomach. "I'm sorry, twin, but you can't be playing with that type of information. Don't you know if something happen to you I ain't no more good?"

Basking in Noni's affection and over-protectiveness, Asha softly replied, "Yeah, I know. And I'm sorry, too. I didn't mean no harm; I was just being childish."

These women crazy, Double-O smirked to himself, then eventually asked Asha if the incidents were related. When she said they were, and told him the names Unique had provided, he instantly thought back to the standoff he had with the two men at D'Aura's funeral. He couldn't remember exactly what he'd promised the one he locked eyes with, but he knew it pertained to him joining the dead— and Double-O prided himself on being a man of his word.

Chapter 13

Inside a strip club called Lips, Hotrod and Dogbite enjoyed a lap dance from two exotic dancers who could've been related. Since being handsomely rewarded for their gas station performance, the men had been making it rain at every lit club in the city. Like the typical clowns who were addicted to being broke, their attention-seeking actions suggested they were in a rush to return to penniless lifestyles.

As the song concluded and the dancers stepped off without once looking back, Hotrod downed a double shot of Hennessey and looked over at Dogbite. "Bro, we need slide to the D," he drunkenly slurred. "I'm getting low on funds, you hear me? I damn near beat my bitch up, 'cause I thought she went in my pockets."

Mentally calculating the balance of his own dwindling funds, Dogbite was thinking along the same lines; as the limelight was costly. "Yeah, we definitely need to do something," he said in agreement. "Because I'm down to like my last eight hunnid."

"You know what else I was thinking," Hotrod leaned closer in a conspiring manner. "We should snatch up Mecca, when she pay us the bread from this next demo. Ain't no way Unique won't pay what we ask. And, nigga, we could shoot for like, two-hunnid thousand, then get the fuck outta dodge, you feel me?"

In spite of his alcohol consumption, Dogbite shook his head in uncertainty. "I don't know, bruh. Them hoes vicious."

"They only vicious because of niggas like us!" Hotrod spat. "I bet ain't neither one of them hoes ever pulled the trigger. All they doing is calling the plays, and we running the routes. So tell me what the fuck so vicious about that."

Though Hotrod had a point, Dogbite couldn't contain his curiosity. "I'm saying, you know I ain't never not had your back, but why all of a sudden you ready to bite this bitch?"

Unwilling to admit it stemmed from the scolding he'd taken from Mecca during their last encounter, Hotrod hotly replied, "Nigga, what the fuck do it matter? This bitch ain't family. And long as I biting on yo' ugly ass, that's all that matters. So, is you down, or what?"

You ain't bit me yet, Dogbite thought, recalling how Mecca was someone Hotrod once worshipped. But to avoid the mistake of appearing distrustful, he agreed to be an accomplice in Mecca's kidnapping. *Then I'm going my own way*, he mentally concluded, glancing at Hotrod out the corner of his eye.

When a different set of dancers approached their table in an attempt to lure them into a private session in the back, Hotrod feigned an attitude to hide the fact that he couldn't afford it. "Damn, bitch, can you see me and my man's chilling right now? Take your thirsty-ass on. Matter fact," he stood up on unsteady legs, "Come on, bro, let's move around. These hoes fooling. Like we ain't just throw a bag in this bitch."

Outside the club, Hotrod staggered beside Dogbite as they walked toward the candy-orange Cutlass. "Aye, bro, won't you let me hold a few hunnid till we put this next demo' down," Hotrod requested. "You know I'm good for it."

You need to sell this dumb-ass car, Dogbite thought, but again agreed to help Hotrod out. "I'ma do it for you, bro, but you gotta make it last. I just told you what I got left, and I still gotta kick my girl half on the rent."

"Nigga, hold the lecture and hand over the bread. We about to be jumping again, and you worried about a few hunnid."

Approaching his car, Hotrod fished the keys from his pocket as he went around to the driver's side.

"Bro, let me drive," Dogbite suggested. "Nigga, you *wet*. You either get us pulled over or wrap this bitch around a pole."

Hotrod held the keys out of reach. "I don't know who scarier, between you or my hoe. I've been driving since I was in diapers, nigga. I can whip this bitch saucy like I can when I'm sober. So get your scary ass in the car and let's go."

As Dogbite wondered how he had put up with Hotrod for so long, he was somewhat relieved when the car wouldn't start.

"What the fuck?" Hotrod cursed in confusion after several failed attempts. "This can't be right. I got oil changes and everything. Bro, won't you hop out and check under the hood real quick."

Dogbite eyed Hotrod as if he couldn't be serious. "Nigga, I ain't no muthafucking mechanic. What the fuck you want me to look under there and do? Your guess just as good as mine on why this bitch won't start."

After several more of Hotrod's unsuccessful attempts at getting the car started, Dogbite had an idea and leaned over. "Look!" He pointed at the dashboard. "You ain't got no gas in this muthafucka, that's why it won't start."

Hotrod shook his head, "Nah, I just filled the tank last night. And I ain't drove nowhere near enough for it to be on E. And I know my girl couldn't have..." He cut his statement short and looked at Dogbite in suspicion. "Bro, you been driving my shit without my knowledge? Because you the only one who got access to my keys."

Not even bothering to waste his breath on a response, Dogbite took out his phone and began scrolling through apps.

"What the fuck is you doing?" Hotrod frowned, to which Dogbite replied,

"Calling a Uber."

Minutes later a white, Ford Fusion pulled into the club's parking lot. *Damn, that was quick*, Dogbite thought as the female-driven car stopped directly behind the Cutlass.

Grabbing a gas can from his trunk, Hotrod joined Dogbite in the Fusion's backseat. "Aye, take us to the gas station," he rudely barked at the driver.

Wearing a dark colored wig and hazel contacts, Kiva turned and smiled, "Right away, sir."

Down the street from the club, Kiva turned on to a one-way and stopped the car in the middle of the block.

"Why the fuck is you stopping?" Hotrod snapped. "I said take us to the gas station."

When Kiva suddenly hopped out the car, Dogbite instinctively looked to his right and froze up at the sight of a hooded figure standing outside his window.

"I'm BFM Noni and this for my sister!" She said before opening fire with a 50-round Draco. After spraying over two dozen rounds into the backseat, Noni lowered the weapon to take in her work.

Responsible for syphoning the gas from Hotrod's car, Double-O appeared alongside his female comrade and coldly suggested, "Let's leave Mecca a message."

***

The area was crawling with cops as Mecca and Unique turned into the plaza where their beauty salon was located. Awakened from their sleep by the authorities, their presence was summoned to what they were told it was a crime scene.

Upon exiting their cream-colored Benz, the first thing they noticed was the shattered front window of the beauty salon.

THE BUTTERFLY MAFIA 4 | FUMIYA PAYNE

THE BUTTERFLY MAFIA 4 | FUMIYA PAYNE

"Excuse me," a well-dressed man walked up, "Are you the two owners of this establishment?"

Mecca said that they were and he introduced himself as Detective Golden, with the Homicide Division. "If you'd follow me, I'd like for you to take a look at something."

Ducking under the yellow crime scene tape, he led them up to the shattered window, stepped aside and extended his hand. "Do you either of you have an idea on why someone would do something like this?"

Neither woman could believe their eyes as they peered into the shop— where the bullet-riddled bodies of Hotrod and Dogbite lay face-up on the floor. Someone had even taken the time to stick a paper to their chest, with the abbreviation written on it in large red letters: R.T.S.

The sisters quickly turned from the window as if repulsed by the sight, with Mecca insisting they knew of no one who would do such a terrible thing.

"And I'm assuming you don't know who either of these men are?" The detective inquired.

Mecca shook her head and convincingly lied, "I don't, detective. Besides taking care of our elderly mother and running this business, me and my sister mainly stay at home. So for something like this to show up on our doorstep is truly disturbing."

While walking the women back to their vehicle, he gave Mecca his card and encouraged them to call if they thought of anything. "And I'll need both of you to stop by my office later, for some follow-up questions."

"Not a problem," Mecca assured him before she got in the car.

Watching the Benz as it drove off, the detective was thinking how the green-eyed woman had done majority of the talking. After making a mental note to question them separately, he returned to the crime scene to search for clues.

Inside the Benz, Mecca banged on the wheel as they idled at a traffic light. "Fuck! These two lil' dumb-ass niggas done let somebody throw them through our fucking front window."

"Mecca, they dead," Unique calmly pointed out. "So I don't think they really had much of a choice."

"Yeah, well, they shouldn't have been doing whatever they was doing that led up to it. And then it's like, why would whoever did it bring that shit to us? Like they were trying to send us some type of message, or something."

Although she was too afraid to reveal her secret meeting with Asha, Unique couldn't leave her sister all the way in the dark. "I think that was a message, Mecca. Didn't you see what that paper on their chests said? The R.T.S.?"

"Of course I saw it. But what's that supposed to stand for?"

Unique looked at her sister and answered, "Return To Sender."

Chapter 14

Escorted by two male security guards, Noni and Double-O were led to Perez's personal skybox at the Detroit Lion's stadium. The drug lord had requested a sit-down, and Noni appeared on Asha's behalf.

When they entered the skybox, Perez's boisterous behavior reminded Noni of the first time her and Asha had met him. Standing at the glass window that overlooked the field, he hurled curses at the ref for what he felt was an unfair call.

"Mr. Centeno, your guests," one of the guards announced during a pause in his tantrum.

Perez partially turned from the window and spoke to no one in particular. "We're finally having a good year, with a real chance to see the playoffs, and our own fucking refs are trying to make sure it doesn't happen. You know, I should make a few calls and get every one of those cocksuckers fired. Or better yet," he looked at his mercenary across the room, "Diablo, I may need you to show them what happens to people who offend me."

With gang graffiti permanently sprayed over his head and face, the MS-13 spoke only one word in return. "Please."

In a wide stance, as he stoically stood with his hands behind his back, Double-O showed no reaction at hearing the underlying threat in their exchange. A loyalist at heart, he'd offend whoever for the Butterfly Mafia; and welcome the aftermath of his actions with open arms.

Smiling to himself as he stepped to the bar, Perez picked up a glass of Patron and twirled it before taking a sip. "Not that it's not nice to see you," he finally addressed Noni, "But where's your sister?"

"Licking her wounds."

Perez nodded, "Yeah, I heard about what happened, and it's very unfortunate. I like Asha, so if you need my help in finding out who did it," he snapped his fingers, "I'll have you a name just like that."

As if she could still taste the blood of her kills, Noni ran her tongue over the diamonds of her teeth. "It's already been taken care of."

He regarded Noni with an unreadable look, then flashed a counterfeit smile that involved only his mouth. "Forgive me, I almost forgot how efficient you can be."

Before Noni could come back with a witty remark, Perez continued, "So here's the thing, I'm sitting on a shit load of stuff that belongs to your sister. As I'm sure you're aware, we have a monthly arrangement. And not to sound insensitive to her situation, but a deal is a deal."

Noni nodded in agreement. "You're absolutely right. And once she's back on her feet, she'll take care of it. But that ain't my lane."

While refilling his glass, Perez replied, "But what I can't understand is, how you can come in here and speak on her behalf, but not act on it. Which leads me to ask, why are you even here?"

As the muscles in Double-O's jaw flexed in anger, his action were observed by the MS-13. He could smell the danger coming off Double-O, and had been watching him closely since he entered the room with a growing desire to demonstrate he was alpha.

"I came as a favor to my sister," Noni answered. "Out of respect, she wanted me to personally let you know that she gon' straighten out her hand. And that's why I'm here."

There was a lapse of silence as the drug lord studied his drink. He could force Noni to take the ball, or he could exercise patience and wait for Asha to recover. As someone who had risen through the ranks by making wise decisions, he went with the latter. "Tell your sister I look forward to seeing her."

The door to the skybox opened and in walked Perez's own sister, Angel. Her eyes darkened at the sight of her former lover. "Why is she here?" Angel demanded of her brother, glaring at Noni.

"Because I didn't know you were coming."

"Well, she needs to leave."

"Gladly," Noni said, avoiding eye contact with Angel as she headed for the door. Since the day Angel angrily exited the twin's birthday party and took back her gifts, Noni hadn't answered or returned any of her many phone calls.

As Double-O followed behind Noni, the MS-13 purposely stepped in his path. "I've literally killed more men than I can even remember," he informed Double-O as they stood face-to-face.

Through marble-like eyes that reflected no fear, Double-O returned his stare with a sinister smile. "That's a lot of bodies, my boy. So because I see this shit like a sport, does that mean that if a man kill you, your body-count becomes his?"

When the gang member failed to immediately respond, Perez intervened to save face for his soldier. "Alright, fellas, that's enough. Diablo, let him pass."

Reluctantly stepping aside, the gang member whispered, "Anytime."

Not one who was big on having the last word, Double-O just smirked and left out the room.

"Bro, you a dangerous, nigga." Noni smiled as they walked down the tunnel.

He smiled back at her. "Why you say that?"

"Because your presence alone had ol' boy tweaking. He stalked you the whole time we was there. Then when he tried to spook you and saw you wasn't going, you really fucked his head up."

"I'm just saying, if two boxers both gotta belts and they fight each other, whoever wins get all the belts, right? So if two killers go at it, and one kill the other, the one still standing should get all the kills. They use gloves in boxing, and we use guns in the streets. But at the end of the day... it's all just a sport."

Noni saw Double-O was dead serious and busted out in laughter. "Yeah, bro, you fried!"

"So, if I'm fried, but you rock with me heavy, then you know what that makes you, right?"

"What?"

"Burnt, gotdammit!" Double-O answered, then joined his best friend in laughter.

***

Later that day...

With Noni behind the wheel and Double-O beside her, they were parked down the street from the shelter where his mother stayed. Shawna continued to insist he give the woman a chance, and Double-O couldn't believe he was actually considering it.

"What you gon' do, brodie?" Noni asked, as he solemnly stared through the demon's front windshield.

He shook his head in uncertainty. "I don't know. I mean, I hear what Shawna saying about people changing, but she don't know what all I went through with this woman. I'm telling you, Noni," returned to face her, "She used to beat me like she wanted me to die. And I can't forget, because the scars won't let me."

"I feel you, my baby," Noni said in solace. "My mama wasn't whooping my ass, but what she did hurt just as bad."

"Yeah?" Double-O said, curious to hear more about his female comrade.

"Yeah, bro. She wanted me to be all girly like Asha, but that was never me. That ain't how I came out. And she made sure to let me know she didn't accept me, every chance she got. She spoiled Asha to death right in front of me. Like, she didn't even try to hide the fact that she ain't fuck with me like that. And if it wasn't for Asha showing me the love she did, I'd probably be in jail right now. Because I'm telling you, O, I used to dream about killing that woman ever night. And it was just a matter of time before it actually happened. But luckily for her, them niggas beat me to it."

As a thoughtful silence trailed their disclosures, the bond between Noni and Double-O just significantly strengthened; for they were two jaded people who personally related to maternal mistreatment.

A subtle smirk appeared on Double-O's face. "Aye, I wonder what God gon' say when we gotta go see Him? Because I already know your ass in trouble. The way you did them niggas in that backseat, that was some Mafia shit for real."

Noni grinned. "Aw, bro, I know you ain't talking, when you the one siphoned that nigga gas. Talking about, 'They gon' have to call a Uber, and all we gotta do is show up'. So if I'm in trouble for my little bitty part, but you the mastermind, then you in way more trouble than me."

"Yeah, well..." He thought of a comeback, "You ain't have to shoot them niggas that many times, either. Now they can't even have a decent funeral, fucking round with your wild ass."

"Nah, nigga," she shook her head, smiling, "You can't even get that one off. Let's not forget, it was your idea to do that Return To Sender shit. All we had to do was dip, but you wanna throw niggas through windows. You was on your John Wick shit, and I'ma need you to take accountability. Because if I gotta go before God, you know I can't lie. I'ma be like, 'God, you know Double-O older than me and supposed to be leading by example. So whatever wrong I did, you gotta blame him for leading me astray'."

Double-O laughed. "And I'ma be like, God, you already know that woman was vicious when I met her. And if you remember, she made me put in work my second day out of the joint."

"Dammmn!" Noni raised her eyebrows in recollection, as she had literally forgot about the murder of the man named Diesel in the projects. "Bro, I cold forgot about that shit. That corny-ass nigga was salty I didn't acknowledge him. You left his shit laying next to that ball. And Lil' Teer helped us rock his ass to sleep."

After another lapse of silence— in which they reflected over things that solidified their friendship, Double-O readjusted himself in the seat and told Noni to pull off.

"You sure, bro?" Noni asked, willing to support whatever decision he made.

Although he wasn't, Double-O nodded and said that he was. "People might do change. But sometimes that shit happen too late, you feel me?"

As Noni drove off, she had no idea his decision had been based with her in mind. Out of a rare allegiance, he didn't want to repair the relationship with his mother, if Noni couldn't do the same with hers. He'd rather share her pain than to let her feel alone. Because in the time he had known her, Noni had showed him more love than his mother had ever— which to him made her worthy of his undying loyalty.

Chapter 15

With the couple's clothing color coordinated, Lo-Lo sat on the trunk of Uno's car, toying with his dreads as he stood between her legs. Accompanied by Guru and other Bandgang members, Uno led his team to falsely believe that it wouldn't be much longer before he had Lo-Lo in a skillet. "We just gotta rock 'em to sleep a lil' while longer," he'd told Lo-Lo in advance to their arrival at the park. "Then, like I said, right after the show, we getting on the road and putting this city in the past."

After Lo-Lo's disheartening visit with Asha she had returned to Uno's apartment and completely broke down. "I don't know what to do," she had cried in his chest, to which he encouraged her to go with her heart. "But you are my heart," she had looked in his eyes, prompting Uno to peel off her pants and sex her so well that she wept for different reasons. As they lay intertwined at the conclusion of their session, Lo-Lo would make the decision to pursue her love life— with or without either of her friend's blessing.

Guru gazed at Lo-Lo out the corner of his eye. This was his first time actually seeing her up close, and he wouldn't deny that the white girl was attractive. But, as a felon who favored wealth over women, he wouldn't hesitate to hurt her if the need arose. The Butterfly Mafia had something he wanted, and Guru was prepared to use Lo-Lo's lover for leverage in order to get it.

"Damn, bro, look!" one man pointed, as a pair of white SUV's coasted through the park. "I think that's them Maybach joints!"

When the two gleaming vehicles came to a stop, so did most conversations of viewers in the vicinity; as they couldn't help but wonder who its occupants were.

As the sunroof of the second SUV retracted, the crisp sound of GloRilla's hood anthem "Yeah Glo" could be heard coming from inside. Then much to the crowd's delight, the Maybach began bouncing like it had hydraulics.

Amid people taking pictures and recording with their phones, the SUV's windows simultaneously lowered and revealed four figures in pink ski masks. With large diamond rings on all four fingers, the driver stuck an arm out the window to use hand gestures while rapping with the song. From the overall visual, the scene resembled a music video.

The ski-masked figures were a sight to behold as they stepped out of the truck. Along with the protection of pink bulletproof vests, they wore layers of diamond chains that radiantly laid over the Teflon material. And judging by the massive butterfly medallion worn by the driver, the crowd had a pretty good idea of who stood in their presence.

Gathering in front of the Maybach's grille, the four figures faced the crowd and began peeling off their masks, one at a time.

First, there was Ray-Ray and Kiva— who some identified as the managers of Club Skittles. Next was Noni— who everyone suspected from the butterfly medallion. But when the fourth and final figure slowly peeled off their mask, a collective gasp escaped from the crowd; as they stared in disbelief at who the city thought was dead— BFM Asha.

"I thought they said she got hit like, ten, fifteen times, bro?" A man on the sideline said to another.

"They did," his crony replied, eyeing Asha in awe. "But clearly it wasn't enough."

As Asha enjoyed being regarded like a ghost, Noni took the spectacle to the next level and climbed on the Maybach's roof— where she stood up on it in her size seven Jordans. With the entire park wondering what she had planned, Noni withdrew a loaf of bread from her pants, popped its rubberband, then yelled out, "BFM for life!" and showered the crowd with nearly ten grand.

While the hands of both sexes seized bills out the air, Asha smiled in amusement as she looked up at Noni. *My baby love her some attention,* Asha thought to herself, but was secretly pleased with her sister's showy stunt.

Inside the lead Maybach was Double-O and two others. Each man in possession of an MP5, their weapons were equipped with armor-piercing rounds. If a person in the park had the heart to make a move, Double-O would ensure they were sent to join Jesus in actual pieces.

In midst of Asha exchanging small talk and fist bumps with various people, Noni walked up and whispered in her ear. When Asha eyed her with a questioning look, Noni bobbed her head in affirmation. "Yeah, twin, *I just* seen it."

Excusing herself from a girl who was interested in working at Skittles, Asha lifted her head at Ray-Ray and Kiva, then, together the four women weaved through the park.

As Double-O was on the verge of losing sight of the girls, he traded the MP5 for a Glock, threw on his hood and hopped out the truck.

With her arms encircled around Uno's neck, Lo-Lo laughed at something he said, when she looked to her left and went stiff as a statue. As if Uno could feel the nervous pounding of her heart, he angled his head to look back at her, and that's when he noticed the source of her fear. Coming in their direction were her four former friends, whose purposeful steps were reflective of their mood.

But as Uno braced himself for some sort of confrontation, the girls marched by without looking his way; as the mission was to simply let their presence be felt.

Lo-Lo dropped her head in shame, wondering if the pursuit of her love life was morally wrong. Those were the girls she loved like sisters, and to see them walk by like strangers didn't sit well with her soul. Though Uno was someone she wanted to marry, she questioned if it was worth the sacrifice of her sisterhood.

From where he stood in the background, Guru focused on the flawless VVS's in the four girls' jewelry as they leisurely strode by. He couldn't believe their audacity, for they were like prancing gazelle's in a predator's presence. As he was tempted to settle for a quick, easy meal, he caught sight of the killer he knew was Double-O. Trailing the girls from several feet back, Double-O had both hands in his hoodie— where Guru didn't doubt was a semiautomatic. *He can't save them forever,* Guru reasoned to himself, and cancelled the idea of a meal no longer easy.

"Y'all see how she couldn't even look at us," Noni pointed out once they returned to the Maybach. "That's how you know she know she wrong."

"Yeah, I can't believe Lo-Lo," Kiva chimed in, slowly shaking her head. "That girl was as solid as they came. But I've seen how women can change, when it comes to certain men. They'll put him before their own kids."

As they continued to comment on Lo-Lo's behavior, Asha studied the ground with a thoughtful expression. While she definitely felt like Lo-Lo betrayed her, Asha began to understand that every woman had a weakness. Recalling Shawna's suggestion on the day she'd gotten shot, Asha thought that maybe it wasn't such a bad idea to make Uno go away; as his death would likely save Lo-Lo's life.

When Asha looked up from the ground, Noni eyed her in a way that implied she knew what her twin was thinking.

What you wanna do? Noni silently asked, to which Asha snuck her a mischievous grin.

You already know. And just like that— without them uttering a word, Uno's fate had been signed, sealed, and on the verge of being delivered.

But if only they would get him before Guru did.

***

A full-size U-haul drove into the Brewster projects— where a number of children noisily played. When the truck rolled to a stop in the center of the complex, people peered through curtains and onlookers stood around; wondering who was moving in or out. But to everyone's surprise, it was Asha and Noni who hopped out of the truck.

"Asha, y'all moving back in?" A little boy ran up to her with a hopeful expression. He could remember a lot of occasions when Asha had rewarded him for doing good in school.

"Nah, not today, Tariq." Asha smiled, running a hand over his braids in affection. "But I got something for you."

He instantly lit up. "Like what!?"

"Come on, let me show you," she said, and led him around to the back of the U-haul.

When her and Noni raised its door, the little boy's eyes nearly bulged out his head. "All this for me?"

"No, this not all for you," Asha laughed, as her and Noni climbed inside. "But you get first dibs."

The U-haul was filled with toys, bicycles, and clothing that ranged in sizes from toddler to teen. With the twins having spent over $50,000, there was enough to bless every girl and boy in the Brewster's.

Once little Tariq walked away with a bike and several outfits draped over the handlebars, it wasn't long before a herd of children were excitedly gathered at the back of the U-haul. It was like an early Christmas for some and the only one for others, and it warmed Asha's heart to see the smiles on their faces. She now offered up prayers on a nightly basis, and this was her way of showing her gratitude to God in regard to her recovery.

Asha and Noni now sat on the edge of the empty enclosure, swinging their legs. "So you ready to *force* Lo-Lo back into the fold, huh?" Noni said, as they watched the children enjoy their new bikes.

Asha nodded. "Yeah, I can't just sit back and let her get mauled by them thirsty-ass wolves. My heart won't allow it. She might hate me in the end, but as long as she safe..." Asha shrugged in contentment, "Then that's all that matters."

"When will it stop, Asha?" Noni looked at her.

"When will what stop?"

"Looking out for everybody, but yourself. Sometimes I think you take this loyalty shit too far."

"Noni, you sound silly right now."

"Nah, no I don't." She shook her head. "Because don't nobody on this earth love you more than me. They can't even come close. And you know I'ma stand behind whatever decision you make, but I just feel like, trying to save Lo-Lo is a mistake. We did it once and look where it got us. And now you want me to do it again?"

"I don't want you to do nothing," Asha sternly corrected her. "Don't forget about Dullah, because I did that alone."

"Yeah, but you didn't have to."

"Shit, after what he did, I didn't have a choice."

Noni frowned. "What you mean, after what he did?"

Inwardly cursing at the slip of her tongue, Asha waved her hand in an attempt to brush it off. "It's water under the bridge, don't worry about it."

"Nah, I wanna know what he did," Noni persisted.

Aside from knowing Noni wouldn't let it go, Asha knew it was time to clear her guilt-ridden conscious. "What happened that night..." she said in reference to the home invasion, "That was Dullah's work. He the one who pushed the button on that shit."

Sensing there was more, Noni waited for Asha to continue. "And he was the one who... told them to do what they did to you."

"What?" Noni eyed Asha in disbelief. "And you just now telling me this? How could you keep something like this from me, twin? When we did we start having secrets?"

"If I would've told you when I first found out, I already know how you would've responded. So I kept it to myself and took care of it. And once it was over, it was like, why even worry you with it? Why get you all upset over something we can't change? I'm so sorry for keeping a secret from you, love. But I did what I knew was in your best interest. Don't nobody on this earth love you more than me, either. And I'll do whatever it takes to protect you from pain."

After the pair partook in a thoughtful silence, Noni looked at her sister. "You know, I can't even be mad at you, twin. Because you right. I would've reacted out of emotion and probably crashed us out. So at the end of the day, they all dead, and that's all that matters."

Although there were more questions Noni wanted to ask, she decided it was best to leave the past in the past. "So, wassup?" She smiled, bumping into Asha. "You ready for your party?"

Asha smiled back. "I'm more excited about Ray-Ray and Kiva. They don't gotta clue on what we about to do."

"They definitely don't," Noni agreed. "And I can't wait to see their faces."

As Asha envisioned an event they would forever remember, she got excited and took Noni's hand. "Come on," she said, jumping down from the U-haul. "We gotta get ready."

After returning the U-haul, Asha had Noni stop by the MGM hotel where they'd previously stayed. "I'll be right back," she said, as Noni double parked the Suburban near the front door.

When Asha entered the hotel and called herself creeping across the lobby, the girl, Symphony, looked up from her desk and literally screamed. "Oh my God!" She exclaimed, hurrying around the desk to wrap Asha in her arms. "It's so good to see you!"

"It's good to see you, too." Asha smiled, despite the woman's bear hug bringing her physical pain.

"Wow," Symphony marvelled, holding Asha at arm's length. "You look just like the same Asha. Like, nothing has changed."

Asha laughed. "That's because it hasn't. They wounded my body, not my spirit. But listen," she said, as Symphony looked back at her desk, "I don't wanna get you in trouble. I just wanted to personally let you know I appreciate you for not saying nothing about us staying here."

"Aw, girl, that was nothing." Symphony waved it off. "I'm just glad I could help. And if there's ever anything else you need, you got my number and you know where to find me."

"Actually, there is something I need. My sister having a party for me later tonight, and I was wondering if you could come through after you got off work. It's right around the corner and you ain't even gotta change."

"Of course I can," she readily answered. "Just text me the addy, and I'll be there as soon as I get off."

Hugging Asha goodbye and assuring her she'd show up, Symphony watched her exit the hotel before going back to work. As she stood behind the desk, she wondered if Asha had texted her the address and reached into pocket of her blazer. "What the hell?" She mumbled, as her hand came into contact with something other than her phone. Upon partially removing it, she saw a thick roll of money was, bound by a rubber band. "That girl something else," she shook her head and smiled, knowing Asha was responsible for sliding it in her pocket.

Asha reentered the Suburban and Noni drove as she reached for her seatbelt. "She said she coming," Asha announced, then played a throwback by Rihanna and settled back in her seat.

"I love you money, I love you money/ I'ma never put a nigga above this money/ I'ma wake up and just hug this money."

-Nothing is Promised-

By means of the interstate, Noni made the thirty-minute trip to their new house in Troy. With the location of Asha's shooting and the hotel so close, the twins had agreed it was time to relocate. So, before Asha's release from the rehab facility, Noni signed a year-long lease on a two-story condo.

"What you over there cheesing at?" Noni smiled at Asha as they got off on their exit.

"It's gon' be a good night, twin," Asha's grin widened. "And I'm telling you, everything about to straighten itself out, I can feel it. We gon' be able to walk away from all this shit. I can't say how, but our lives about to change in a way we never expected."

Little did she know how true her statement was; for in just a few short weeks they'd be placed in a position only God could've predicted.

***

Upon the twins arrival at Club Skittles that night, they pulled into a parking lot that was already packed. Ray-Ray and Kiva were the party promoters, and the two women excelled at attracting large crowds.

As they walked across the parking lot, a car door opened and Asha was surprised by the passenger that appeared. "Shawna?"

Instantly tearing up at the sight of her big sister, Shawna bobbed her head, "Yeah, it's me."

121

"Girrrrl," Asha hurried to hug her, "What you doing here?"

"I had to see you, Asha," her tears began falling. "It's been almost two months and I miss you so much."

"I miss you, too, love, but you know we've been talking on the phone almost every other night."

"But it's not the same as seeing you in person. So I just had to come hug you. And I made Double-O do it, so don't mad at him for bringing me."

The girls broke apart and Asha used her thumbs to erase Shawna's tears. "You such a big baby."

"You know I can't help it."

There was a knock on the car window and they turned to see a bright-eyed Polaris waving at Asha.

"Hey, pretty mama!" Asha opened the backdoor and reached in to pick her up. "How you been doing, baby?"

As Polaris answered she was fine, Bella stood on the seat and barked for her return; for Asha was a stranger to the overprotective pup.

"Alright, alright," Asha laughingly returned the little girl to her dog. "I don't want no beef with you, Bella."

"Yeah, I forgot to tell you about that," Shawna said as Asha closed the backdoor. "That dog don't play when it come to Polaris. She follow her everywhere, and she even sleep in the bed with her at night."

Asha looked at Noni with a proud-like smile, as it was her idea to give a canine companion to the traumatized child.

After conversing with Shawna a few minutes longer, Asha hugged her again and instructed her to leave. "Alright, gone and get up out of here, and I'll call you later. And don't worry, everything finna fall perfectly in place. I just need you to stay safe."

As the twins watched the Porsche pull off, Noni voiced her inner thoughts. "You really got faith in that girl, don't you?"

"That goes without question," Asha emphatically answered. "And you should feel the same. Because I can't say how it'll happen, but I promise you, Noni, in the end it's gon' be Shawna that keep the ship from sinking."

When they entered their club, the crowd greeted Asha with cheers and applause. As the female DJ gave her a shout-out, Asha took in the 'Welcome Back' banners that hung along the walls. It had been a minute since she last stepped foot inside Skittles, but the building she designed still felt like home.

"Wassup, young Queen?" Someone addressed Asha from behind, to which she turned to see it was her Chief of Security. "Aw, hey, Bolo!" She beamed in response, giving him a light hug. "I heard you been holding it down in here, player."

He downplayed the praise with a nonchalant shrug. "I've been managing. Just doing what I would do as if you were here. But seriously, though, Asha, it's good to have you back. And if there's *anything* you need, consider it already done."

Asha nodded in gratitude. "I appreciate that, Bolo. And I meant what I said about you holding it down. We all play a role in here, and yours is just as important as anyone else's. So don't ever think I'd take your integrity for granted."

Exchanging hugs and pleasantries with patrons and employees, Asha made her way towards a VIP booth— where Ray-Ray and Kiva stood among ice-filled buckets of champagne bottles.

"Welcome back!" They greeted, giving her a hug and a kiss on the cheek.

As the four women sat around the table, sipping and snickering, the DJ lowered the music to make an announcement. "I'ma need everybody to stop what they doing and put their hands together for BFM Noni!" she said, then shined a spotlight over the girls' table. "She got her first professional fight coming up at the Huntington Center in Toledo, and we already know she gon' put on for the city.

123

Which is why I got free tickets for everybody in here tonight. We gon' show up and show our support!"

At the crowd's loud reaction, a surprised Noni looked around the table, wondering which woman was responsible.

"It was us," Kiva confessed, referring to Ray-Ray and herself. "It was the least we could do to show our appreciation."

Ray-Ray raised her glass to propose a toast. "Here's to Noni's first fight as a professional boxer."

Clinking their glasses, they downed their drink and Kiva exclaimed, "And, Noni, you better beat that bitch ass, whoever she is!"

Feeling the thrilling effects of her alcohol consumption, Asha quietly surveyed the electrifying scenery inside the club. The moment felt magical. Despite whatever problems people had in their lives, none of it mattered in that present space of time. But at the close of her survey, Asha was saddened by the absence of someone who should've been present— BFM Lo-Lo.

Asha was so deep in thought, that she wasn't immediately aware of Noni waving for her attention.

"Damn, twin, wassup?" Noni asked once she saw Asha's focus return to reality.

"I'm good," she smiled. "I just got caught up in the moment, that's all."

Asha's phone then buzzed on the table from an incoming text. She read the message and looked toward the entrance, where a lady soon walked in with a small, toolbox. "Come on, she here," Asha nudged Noni and rose from the table.

"Aye, y'all come with us right quick," Noni told Ray-Ray and Kiva as she exited the booth. The friends exchanged a look as they rose to their feet, wondering if they were about to be demoted now that Asha was back.

With all five women gathered in the back room, Asha looked at Ray-Ray and Kiva. "Good energy is something either you got, or you don't. You can't fake it. So a person can tell you anything, but if you know how to read it, their energy will tell you how they really feel about you."

As Ray-Ray and Kiva grew concerned, Asha's next words brought them inner relief. "Since the moment we met, your energy hasn't once given off bad vibes. So I can honestly say that I'm happy to have helped add value to your lives. And I salute your ambition. I salute you for stepping up to an open position. Because if it's one thing I know, strong women get ahead and the weak make excuses. So, with that being said, me and twin was just wondering, is y'all trying to get down with this Mob shit, or what?"

"Hell yeah!" They exclaimed in unison.

"Girl, we been wanting to get down with y'all for a minute now," Kiva revealed. "But some shit gotta be organic, you feel me?"

It was Kiva's assistance in the Flint homicides that solidified the twins' decision to bring them on board. They two women had watched over Polaris, taken care of the club, and even risked their freedom— on the sole strength of loyalty.

"Alright, let's make it official, then," Noni said, to which the woman opened her toolbox to reveal a tattooing kit.

Ray-Ray got her BFM stamp on the right side of her neck, while Kiva got 'Butterfly Mafia' across her collarbone. And though the pieces were different, you could tell by the quality they were professionally done.

After the tattooist had left and the artwork was admired, Asha smiled at the two new members and opened her arms, "Welcome to the Mob."

Chapter 16

Three blacked-out Suburbans sped down I-75. It was the day of Noni's fight and the vehicles were en route to the Huntington Center in Toledo, Ohio.

Inside the lead SUV, Kiva had the wheel and Asha rode shotgun. Seated behind them was Ray-Ray, Shawna, Polaris, and Noni sat in the last row with her headphones on and her eyes closed. Covered in diamonds, each woman wore layers of sparkling BFM chains, while Polaris sported a child-size Cuban with a butterfly medallion.

In the center SUV was Noni's coach and her training camp; and bringing up the rear was Double-O and two men who were willing to commit murder in front of a police precinct.

Arriving at the Huntington Center— where they pulled into a reserved section of its parking garage, a security team escorted Noni and her entourage to her private dressing room.

"How you feeling, champ?" Coach Bell asked Noni as he unpacked one of her bags. "Because it's okay to be nervous."

"Nervous? Coach, I'm about to make this look easier than a walk in the park."

At Noni's cocky response, Coach Bell asked for everyone to step out the room so he could have a word with his fighter. Once him and Noni were alone, he went in. "I pulled every string I had to make this match happen. So what we not gon' do is take it for granted. Save that cocky shit for the gym, Noni, because this ain't the place or time for it."

"Coach, I was just –"

"You was just nothing," he sharply cut her off. "Noni, you gotta go in that ring with the understanding that anything can happen. All it takes is one lucky punch to cut the power off, and I've seen it happen to the best of them. And the only way to prevent that from happening tonight, is by going out there and fighting your opponent like you fighting for your life. The stage is set, now it's all up to you on how you'll perform. And I'm not saying don't be confident, I'm just saying make sure you balance it with carefulness. You understand me, Noni?"

She solemnly nodded and he placed his hands on her shoulders. "If you wasn't special, I wouldn't be wasting either of our time. You naturally got what some train years to attain, and others will forever fall short of. I've watched hours of film on the best fighters in this division, and none of them could outbox you on their best day and your worst. Many are called but few are chosen, Noni. So let's stay focused and be the one the few who plant their flag at the top. Let's put the world on notice that Noni is here... and that it's just a matter of time before the crown is awarded to its rightful owner."

With everyone back in the dressing room, Noni now wore boxing attire as she hit the mitts with Coach Bell. In harmony with her character, her outfit was flashy and predominantly pink. She wore a pair of boxing shoes by Jordan, a glittery kilt-like ensemble over her spandex shorts, and a pink and white sports bra that matched her gloves. With her braids arranged in a unique design, she looked more ready for a photoshoot than an actual fight.

As Coach Bell called out combos off the top of his head, Noni executed each with a crisp delivery. "There you go, Noni," he praised as she doubled up her jab. "And I want you to watch for the overhand right," he said in reference to her opponent's favorite punch. "She slow to bring it back every time she throws it. So I just need you to slip it, go low to the body, then come straight back up top with a right hand, left hook."

There was a knock at the door and a man poked his head in to announce Noni's fight was soon coming up. "You got about forty-five minutes till your ring walk."

After wishing Noni good luck and giving her hugs, the girls left the room to let her and coach Bell make final preparations. While headed to their ring-side seats— where they'd join Double-O, Asha lagged back from the group to make a quick phone call. "Come on, girl, pick up," she mumbled to herself as Lo-Lo's number rang.

***

Uno was turning into the parking garage of his apartment, when Lo-Lo got the call from Asha. She signaled for him to be quiet and answered in an uncertain tone, "Hello?"

"If you ready to come back home, then I suggest you get your ass to Toledo, ASAP," Asha said, bypassing pleasantries. "Noni, about to have her first fight at the Huntington Center, and if you leave right now you'll make it."

"Is she cool with it?"

"Lo-Lo, if you don't stop wasting time and get your ass on the road. And call me when you get here."

As Uno parked beside her Stingray Corvette, Lo-Lo brightened at the idea of a reunion with her girls. "Alright, I'm on my way."

After her recent run in with Asha and the others at Belle Isle, Lo-Lo concluded she made a mistake by placing a man over the Mob. Those were the women who stood by her side through the harshest conditions. Unwilling to walk away from friendship founded on loyalty, she had just broke the news to Uno over dinner that she needed some time to herself.

"I'm about to go to Noni's fight," Lo-Lo informed Uno upon hanging up with Asha. "But I'll definitely call you when I get back, because there's something we need to talk about."

Wondering what it was, Uno just nodded in response. "Alright. And just know that regardless of what happens, my feelings won't change. I'ma still love you then, as much as I do now.

Lo-Lo gave him a peck on the lips and exited the car. As she reached for the door of her burnt-orange coupe, she turned at the sound of squealing tires.

An SUV sped up and screeched to a stop, blocking in Lo-Lo and Uno's cars. The passenger doors opened, and a pair of masked hooligans hopped out the truck, bearing mini assault rifles. As proof that their weapons were operable, one of the gunman let off a burst of rounds at an upwards angle.

As Lo-Lo crouched down alongside her car, she was more concerned with letting down her girls than the safety of her life. Along with knowing she would miss Noni's fight, she knew she would probably never see them again.

***

Surrounded by her team as she walked to the ring, a robe-wearing Noni came out to the music of her favorite female artist, Young M.A. While bobbing her head to the song called 'No Mercy', she flashed her diamond teeth at different people in the crowd— mainly women. With 4,000 in attendance, Noni was consumed with a euphoric feeling.

When the beat dropped, Noni stopped to lock eyes with a caramel-colored doll and rapped, "Cameras out, hold up, let me pose/ pretty muthafucka, put me on the front of Vogue/ this about to be the greatest story never told..."

With her infectious energy infecting the crowd, Noni had women and men mirroring her movements. Halfway down the aisle, she spotted a section of the crowd that made her proudly smile and offer a salute. Wearing clothing that represented their Motor City origin, natives of her city had indeed showed up to show their support.

As her gloves were inspected and a coat of Vaseline was applied to her face, Noni searched out her sister and slipped her a wink. *I got this, love*, she silently assured Asha.

Coach Bell split the ropes and Noni entered the ring, where her opponent was present in the opposite corner. She was a Philippine fighter with an impressive record of thirteen wins and only one loss.

Once her robe was removed— revealing the Butterfly tattoo that covered the majority of her back, Noni bounced in place and sized up her opponent with a predatory glare. This was her moment, and she had every intention on making the most of it.

When the ring announcer introduced her to the crowd as Noni 'The Don' Kincaid, the Detroit section especially turned up, chanting in unison, "BFM Noni."

At the volume of their chant, Asha had an outbreak of goosebumps on her arms. She was so proud of her Noni and would do everything in her power to progress her career. And she would start by ending the arrangement with Perez. Once she relieved him of this last shipment, she'd inform him of her decision to discontinue dabbling in such a dangerous game. Club Skittles did numbers, and the daycare would soon open; which made it foolish to continue with unnecessary risks.

The bout got underway, and Asha sat on the edge of her seat in nervous anticipation— for she was utterly fearful of seeing her sister lose. She knew Noni could fight, but her opponent was someone with professional experience. *Get her, Noni,* Asha encouraged her.

As if Asha had just spoken directly in her ear, Noni slipped a punch from her opponent and countered with a crispy combo that excited the crowd. However, near the end of the round Noni lowered her guard and caught a vicious right hand, flush on her chin. But as Noni grabbed her opponent to prevent her from throwing additional punches, she looked at Coach Bell and smiled.

At the close of the round Noni returned to her corner and waved off the stool in refusal to sit. "Noni, what I tell you about dropping your hands!" Coach Bell snapped upon removing her mouthpiece.

"Coach, listen to me," Noni pleadingly replied, "On my sister, she can't fuck with me. I just ate her hardest punch. I can run straight through her, coach, I promise you."

He gauged her closely. "You sure?"

"I'll walk home if I ain't."

Smirking in response, he decided to let Noni place her fate in her own hands. "Alright, well... I wasn't gon' tell you this, but my wife just texted me and said dinner ready. So get us out of here, Noni, so I can go home and eat."

"Say less," she said before he reinserted her mouthpiece.

Noni's plan was simple, she'd take a little to give a whole lot. She would lure her opponent into launching an offensive attack, then she'd counter with a flurry that would undoubtedly do damage. And once her opponent stood on unsteady legs, she would finish her off with a leaping left hook.

Midway through the fourth, Asha jumped to her feet as Noni leaned against ropes and absorbed power punches. She was seconds from shouting for Noni to move, when to the crowd's delight, the tables suddenly turned.

Noni slipped left to avoid a right hand, then gracefully pivoted and pinned her opponent in the corner. Slightly stepping back to get within perfect range, Noni showcased her precision and power through a series of shots. Having the ability to see action play out in slow motion, she saw her opening and unloaded with the leaping left hook.

In a surreal moment, Noni heard the crowd's eruption as her opponent fell face forward onto the canvas. She wanted to scream and jump around in celebration, but instead she calmly retreated to a neutral corner.

When the referee waved off the bout— as the woman was clearly unconscious, Noni and her coach gripped each other in a fierce embrace. "I told you you were special!" He said in her ear, to which a teary-eyed Noni just nodded in response. For the first time in her life she had achieved an accomplishment that would bring her sister joy. Noni loved herself but loved Asha even more, and her purpose in life was just to make her sister proud.

As Noni received hugs and congrats from the members of her team, she was summoned to the center of the ring for an interview. After having her explain what was going through her mind in the final seconds of the fight, the announcer asked her if she had any comments for the crowd.

Noni angled to where she faced her sister. "First and foremost, I wanna give a shout out to my twin. I did this for you, mama. Because without you I wouldn't be in this ring right now. So from the bottom of my heart, I cherish you, love. To the Butterfly Mafia and my boy Double-O, we might not be blood but we related through loyalty. And to my people from the 'D' who showed up in support, I double salute you for standing behind me. We from that Murder Mitten, my baby!"

Amid cheers from her natives, the announcer asked Noni what viewers could expect to see from her in the future. She stared into a camera and answered, "You can expect to see me put more heads to bed than a daycare. I'm Noni 'The Don'. And whether you love me or judge me, either way won't change what I'm destined to do. BFM for life!"

It wasn't until Noni returned to her dressing room did her and Asha hug and start jumping up and down while hysterically screaming. "You did it!" Asha exclaimed, shedding tears of joy.

When the twins broke apart, Asha's eyes rolled upwards, her body locked up and she collapsed to the floor and began wildly convulsing. "What the fuck?" Noni said, frozen in shock at the startling sight.

"She's having a seizure!" Coach Bell said as he sprung into action. "Somebody call 9-1-1."

Ray-Ray reached for her phone, and Kiva motioned for Shawna to take the child out of the room.

Not knowing what to do, Noni watched in horror as Asha's convulsing body was rolled on its side in an effort to prevent her from swallowing her tongue. She couldn't believe how a dream come true could so suddenly convert into a living nightmare.

By way of EMT, Asha was rushed to a nearby hospital. While everyone else prayerfully gathered in a group, Noni sat alone in a corner with her head down. *This all my fault*, she blamed herself, vowing not to ever touch another pair of gloves.

As they sat around in suspenseful silence, Polaris asked Shawna, "Do Auntie Asha gotta go to heaven?"

The volume of her voice made Shawna glance in Noni's direction— who displayed no reaction to the little girl's question. Shawna returned her attention to Polaris. "No, baby, Auntie Asha don't gotta go to heaven. She just got a little sick, that's all."

Polaris considered her response and replied, "I wanna go check on Bella. I wanna make sure she not sick, too."

Before Shawna could tell her she'd have to wait, Ray-Ray spoke up. "I think that's a good idea. Matter fact," she looked at Coach Bell, "If you could drop them off at home, we'd really appreciate it. Because there's really no need for us all to be here. And Shawna, we'll let you know something as soon as we do. Now take that baby home so she can check on her puppy."

Shawna didn't want to leave, but knew it was in the child's best interests. So she reluctantly agreed, but first made them promise to call her the second they spoke with a doctor.

Shortly after Shawna left, a doctor came out to inform them of Asha's condition. "She's back to normal, but, as a result of her recent head trauma, I'm afraid she'll have a recurrent disorder of the nervous system."

"And what exactly does that mean?" Kiva irritated asked. She hated how doctors used medical terms as if regular people should know what they meant.

"It means, there's medicine she can take, but it's likely your friend will have seizures for the remainder of her life."

Still alone in the corner, Noni dropped a fresh set of tears at the disheartening news. She just couldn't understand how someone like Asha— who was so pretty and pure-hearted, always encountered adversity.

Per policy, Asha's discharge from the hospital included a wheelchair departure. As Ray-Ray rolled her out, with Noni and Kiva at her side and Double-O trailing, Asha looked up at her sister's sullen expression. "Noni, why you looking like they told you I'm dead?"

With a subtle shake of her head, Noni quietly replied, "I don't know, twin, that shit just fucked me up. And now the doctor talking about you might have seizures for the rest of your life."

"Well, look on the bright side," Asha smiled, taking Noni's hand.

"And what's that?"

"That means you gotta stay by my side and watch over me for the rest of my life."

Chapter 17

Nursing a bottle of wine that was nearly empty, Angel sat on the floor in the living room of her house. She had secretly attended Noni's fight— in hopes that she lost, and her victory had heightened the degree of Angel's hatred. She hated Noni for making her fall in love. She hated Noni for throwing her away once she was no longer useful. She hated Noni for ignoring her phone calls. But most of all, she hated Noni for appearing to be happy, while she on the other hand drowned in sadness.

"Who does she think she is?" Angel slurred to herself. "That black bitch! Acting as if she can't be punished. And like I can't be the one that do it."

She rose to her feet and staggered over to a mirror. "You're Angel Centeno. You're not a pushover, you're a princes. And whoever don't agree, you gotta make them pay. And starting with Noni. Make that black bitch pay!"

Overcome with emotion, Angel hurled the bottle at the 80-inch television mounted on the wall. As both the bottle and screen shattered upon impact, Angel was consumed by an intoxicating rage that drove her to destroy everything within reach. She even threw the vase that contained her father's ashes through the front window.

With there being nothing left to break as she panted in exhaustion, Angel went into her room— where her fury transformed to self-pity and she sank to her knees and loudly sobbed.

"Angel?" Her brother, Perez, called in alarm as he entered her ransacked house. She hadn't been answering the phone for him or their mother, and he decided to stop by to ensure she was safe.

Armed with a pistol as he peered into her bedroom, Perez saw her on the floor, returned the weapon to his waist and rushed to embrace her. "What's wrong?"

She hugged him tightly and cried, "I hate her, I hate her, I hate her."

Knowing she referred to Noni, he understood only time could heal heartbreak. But in support of his sister, he decided it was best to break off business with Asha; as their dealings were now a conflict of interests.

Perez picked up his sister and laid her in bed. "I can smell you've been drinking, and you need to sleep it off. But I give you my word, after this last deal I got coming up with Asha, I'm cutting off their water. So you'll never have to worry about bumping into them again. Now get some rest, while I have someone come and clean up this place."

Once her brother had left and she lay alone in the dark, Angel's eyes snapped open at a sudden idea. She played with the pieces until they formed a perfect picture, then cunningly smiled; for she now had a way to make Noni pay.

Chapter 18

In the basement of a boarded-up house, Uno and Lo-Lo were tied to separate chairs that sat facing each other. His right eye was swollen, which resulted from his resistance in the parking garage.

As the two masked gunman stood guard, a third man— the driver— sat a chair between his hostages and took a seat. When he removed his mask, Uno was hardly surprised their abductor was Guru. "You know my voice, and we're past playing games."

"Bro, I told you I had it under control. But this right here..." Uno said in reference to him being kidnapped, "Come on, 'Ru, how could you do this to *me*? When I've never done *nothing* to harm your well-being."

Guru smirked. "You might be a better rapper than me, I'll give you that. But when it come to this street shit, you a whole lot of steps behind, my baby. I read niggas like I wrote their story myself. And with yours, I just had to skip a few chapters and read the part where you planned on dipping after we did the show. You thought you being the better rapper would buy you some time. But you overlooked one thing, Uno...I'ma rapper second and a Savage first."

While Uno maintained a blank expression, he was actually appalled at Guru's ability to predict his intentions. Instead of playing with fire, he should've fled the scene at the first sign of smoke.

"So here's what I'ma do," Guru continued, "I'ma give your girl a chance to rewrite the story. Because the ending I came up with," Guru shook his head at the grizzly thought of it, "I don't think y'all gon' like it at all. But I'm telling you now, if she don't tell me what I wanna hear, ain't gon' be no riding off into the sunset. Nah, it's gon' be two dead-ass bodies down here in this basement."

Guru angled his head in Lo-Lo's direction. "I already know about y'all buildings. How y'all switch up locations, every thirty days, all that. But what I don't know is where y'all hiding all that chicken at. So all you gotta do is tell me where it's at, I'ma go check to make sure you being truthful, then you and this tender-dick-ass nigga can get back to y'all plans."

"I can tell you where it's at, but you not gon' like the answer," Lo-Lo replied.

"Try me."

"It's at PNC."

Guru frowned. "PNC?"

"Yeah, PNC, the bank. That's where all the money at."

He chuckled at the location. "Come on, you can't expect me to believe y'all hauling all that drug money up in no muthafucking bank. Y'all selling more dope than anybody I know, and PNC just letting y'all walk up in they shit and deposit all them illegal-ass profits? That's what you want me to believe?"

"That's the truth," Lo-Lo affirmed, which it was for the most part.

Guru slowly shook his head in growing frustration. "I can't understand why you making this difficult. White girl, please believe me when I tell you I've killed plenty for pennies. You in a lose-lose, I promise you. So the sooner you tell me where it's at, the sooner we can part ways."

"I don't know what else you want me to tell you," Lo-Lo said. "And I can't understand why you can't wrap your mind around the answer I've given you. Just because you haven't figured out how to get your money in the bank, doesn't mean the next person hasn't."

"You know what? You right," Guru pointed at her. "You absolutely right. So I'ma make this even more simple for you. Just tell where the twins live, and we even. I can go have this conversation with them. Because I already know which one in charge. Matter fact," he looked at Uno and slyly crossed his fingers, "If this bitch tell me where they live, on my dead mama I'll let y'all go. And Uno, you know I ain't never lied on my mama."

Uno knew that was true, which was why his good eye looked at Lo-Lo with a questioning expression; as if asking, what you wanna do?

Being watched by three eyes, Lo-Lo truthfully stated, "After Asha got shot, they moved out the city. And other than their landlord and God, don't nobody know where."

Bobbing his head, as he now understood what had to be done, Guru scooted his chair back and rose to his feet. He was finished playing games and would go to plan B— using her lover as leverage.

Without warning, Guru hit Uno square on the jaw, breaking the bone in the process. And he repeatedly struck him until Uno lost consciousness. When he turned to see Lo-Lo had her eyes tightly shut, Guru pulled out his pistol and cocked back the slide. "Bitch, open your eyes."

When Lo-Lo complied, she gasped at the sight of Uno's disfigured face.

"You did this," Guru codly accused. "And you the only one who can stop it. So you gotta decide between love for this nigga, or loyalty to them bitches. But if you close your eyes again," he levelled the gun with Uno's swollen head, "I'ma make the decision for you."

Returning the weapon to the small of his back, Guru slapped Uno awake. "Get your bitch-ass up, nigga. Your hoe seems to think you ain't had enough yet."

As an agonizing moan escaped through Uno's split lips, Guru punished his midsection until he threw up.

"Lo-Lo, please!" Uno begged, although he couldn't see her through either swollen eye. "Please make it stop."

With tears streaming down her face, Lo-Lo bit back a sob. It broke her heart to see Uno reduced to such a pitiful state. He broke her heart to hear him beg for a life that was already gone.

"Uno, I'm sorry," she finally addressed his pitiful plea. "But there's nothing I can say that'll make him stop hurting you."

Lo-Lo may not have known where the twins lived, but she did know the location of the stash house in Pontiac. But she'd rather be buried in that basement than to betray Asha's trust— even if it included the death of the fetus in her belly. Unbeknown to Uno or her friends, Lo-Lo had recently learned she was six weeks pregnant. *It might not be Uno's teeth that bite you, but, Lo-Lo, I promise you gon' get bit.* Those were Asha's words that replayed in her mind. And because she didn't listen, she would never get the chance to become what she had dreamed of— a better mother than her own.

After he beat Uno to within an inch of his life, a winded Guru looked at Lo-Lo and panted, "You don't think I'll kill this nigga, do you? You don't think I'll spray this nigga shit all over your face?"

Guru went behind Uno's chair and pushed it forward until their knees collided. He then stepped back, pointed the pistol at Uno's head and gave Lo-Lo one last chance to save her lover's life. "Where that shit at?"

Who are you? Lo-Lo heard Asha ask her, which pertained to the creed of the Butterfly Mafia. And Lo-Lo heard herself answering in a tone of conviction, *My Sister's Keeper.*

Lo-Lo returned Guru's gaze and boldly rebelled, "You can beat me, rape me, or whatever, but it's not gon' change what I've already told you."

140

Guru smirked, pursed his lips and fired. As promised, he framed Lo-Lo's face with Uno's blood and brain fragments. "You lucky that bullet didn't go straight through," he said, stepping from behind Uno's lifeless body. "So, you still standing on that answer?"

Sickened by the slimy feel of what covered her face, Lo-Lo spit out what could've been a piece of Uno's brain. "If you think I'ma beg, you got the wrong white girl."

"Yeah, I definitely misjudged you," Guru admitted, regarding Lo-Lo in a totally different light. "And I think you making the same mistake right now."

He walked out of sight and reappeared a moment later with a red gallon jug. "Here, let me clean off your face," he crudely joked and splashed her with its contents.

It took Lo-Lo just a split second to make out the smell—gasoline. This barbarian intended to burn her alive.

As Guru continued to douse her, Lo-Lo thought about her little brother, Lance. She'd never get the chance to see his precious face again. He was so timid and naive, and she could only pray he'd find his place in the world. But as painful as it was to forsake her younger sibling, Lo-Lo understood that she had made her bed, and it was now time to lay in it.

Pouring a trail of gasoline as he backpedaled to the steps, Guru tossed the empty jug and pulled a lighter from his pocket. "Any last words?"

Horrified at what would be a tortuous death, Lo-Lo remembered the Butterfly Mafia's oath. *In my sister shall I trust, from my sister shall I learn. To her aid shall I rush... and for each other shall we burn.*

In her refusal to grant Guru any satisfaction, Lo-Lo put on her game face and bravely declared, "BFM for life!"

"As you wish," he coldly replied before flicking the lighter and releasing it. At the sound of Lo-Lo's piercing screams, Guru and his two henchmen headed upstairs.

"What we gon' do now, 'Ru?" one of the men asked, pulling off his mask as they exited the house.

Guru's wicked response sent chills through the man. "We gon' barbeque bitches till one of them talk."

Chapter 19

All five members of the Butterfly Mafia— including Polaris and Bella, were gathered in the parking lot of Big Baby's daycare. The building's renovation was officially complete, and the women took a moment just to soak it all in. Beautifully painted in pink and blue colors, it reflected the inviting appearance of a child-friendly daycare.

"Shawna, you did your thing, girl," Ray-Ray complimented with the nodding of her head. "If I had kids, I'd wanna bring them here off just the outside look alone."

Shawna couldn't stop smiling, as she was pleased by their compliments and the completion of her project. Never had she dreamed she'd achieve such a fulfilling accomplishment. And to think, there had been so many nights she wanted to give up on life. If there was one word of advice she could give someone else who struggled in life, it was that, 'there wouldn't be rainbows if it wasn't for rain'.

"Wow!' Was Kiva's stunned reaction upon their entering the daycare. "I wasn't expecting all this."

Beneath their feet was thick carpet, so when children fell it would soften the impact. Along with separate sleeping rooms for girls and boys, there were twin-size beds for each individual child. There was a large game room, which was stocked with more than enough toys and games. And in the dining room area, there were a number of highchairs for infants, and a long square table where everyone would eat as a family. Shawna's goal had not only been to provide an affordable place for parents to bring their children, but to provide a loving, family-like structure for those who might've lacked one at home. And in doing so, just maybe Big Baby's would have a positive impact on one those children's lives.

"Yeah, a lot of kids ain't gon' wanna go home after seeing this," Ray-Ray said. "This ain't no regular daycare. And you even got them with their own beds."

"When this joint supposed to open?" Kiva asked.

As Shawna answered she was still in process of finding the right employees, Noni noticed Asha was distracted by her phone. Since the night of her seizure, Asha had been different, and Noni could sense it. And though she couldn't pinpoint exactly what it was, she was certain it had something to do with Lo-Lo.

Asha felt Noni watching her as she typed a text message. And her sister was right, with regard to Lo-Lo being the source of her concern. After she failed to show up to Noni's fight, Asha couldn't help but wonder if something went wrong. There was always the chance Lo-Lo had chosen to stay with Uno, but she could at least let it be known she was somewhere safe.

In celebration of Shawna's achievement, the girls ordered pizza for themselves and McDonald's for Polaris. While waiting for the food to arrive, Asha got a text and was disappointed to see that it wasn't from Lo-Lo. She slipped Noni a subtle head gesture, then announced to the others they had to run a quick errand.

"Y'all good?" Kiva asked, as she, too, sensed Asha was troubled by something.

Asha tried to mask her anxiety with a halfhearted smile. "We good, love. We'll be right back."

As Shawna watched them leave, Asha looked at her in a way she wouldn't comprehend until later in life.

With Noni driving, the twins drove from the daycare to their club and parked around back. The text Asha just received came from Double-O, who would soon pull up with a dump truck full of drugs.

In recently speaking with Perez, Asha was relieved when he told her this would be their last deal. "It's nothing against you, but in the best interests of my sister," he'd told her in person. As that was exactly in line with what Asha desired, she told Perez she understood and genuinely thanked him for the golden opportunity.

Noni checked the time and looked at Asha, "What's going on? Why you so worried about Lo-Lo?"

Her twin knew her so well, Asha thought to herself. "She was supposed to come to your fight and never showed up. And we both know Lo-Lo ain't no liar."

"So let's slide by her spot," Noni suggested. Unlike last time, when she doubted her sister about D'Aura being in danger, Noni would take heed to Asha's intuition.

"But we gotta wait on Double-O," Asha replied, although tempted to tell Noni to take off right then. But because they were hiding this last shipment themselves, she didn't want him to show up and they hadn't made it back.

"It's gon' be at least an hour before he get here," Noni pointed out, putting the truck in drive. "So we got plenty of time to slide by her spot real quick."

When Noni turned out the club, in the opposite direction of where Lo-Lo stayed, Asha was confused. "Noni, where you going?"

"Aw, I gotta stop by the house and pick up a new toy," Noni replied with a devilish smile. "If Lo-Lo ain't home, I forgot to tell you... I know where that nigga, Uno, live at."

***

Parked down the street from an abandoned warehouse, Double-O watched one of his men throw several duffel bags over into the bed of a dirt-filled dump truck, then climb in behind them. A minute later he climbed back out, dusted his clothing, climbed in the passenger seat and the truck rumbled off. With kilos of heroin and pounds of crystal meth hidden beneath the dirt, the truck was en route to the rear of Club Skittles.

Once the truck reached the corner, Double-O was on the verge of pulling off behind it, when law enforcement swarmed in from everywhere. Hopping out of unmarked vehicles with tactical weapons, FBI agents surrounded the truck and ordered the driver to turn off the ignition.

As Double-O slid lower in his seat, so as not to be seen, he was grateful for going with his gut instinct earlier.

In the past, Double-O had driven the truck himself. But after a forewarning that morning from his intuition, he reached out to two solid teens from Teer's former team. And despite feeling guilty over their present predicament, he found comfort in knowing they wouldn't be sentenced too harshly— for the two suspects ahead were juvenile offenders. Still a student of the game, he had taken a page out of Asha's playbook.

Afraid to pull off, for fear of attracting unwanted attention, Double-O sent Asha a warning text message. *They cancelled the game over cherries and berries.* With cherries and berries being Noni's favorite term for police, he knew they'd decipher the message and immediately get missing.

While watching the two handcuffed boys be sat in separate SUVs, Double-O wondered who ratted them out. And as common sense prevailed, it said the rodent was related to Perez.

***

Just as Double-O's warning text came through on Asha's phone, Noni exited their house with a green army bag. *What the hell this girl got?* Asha wondered to herself, as she now sat behind the wheel.

When Noni reentered the Suburban she smiled at her sister's disapproving expression. "What?"

"Noni, what you done went in there and got?"

"It's my new toy. Like I said, if Lo-Lo ain't home we gon' go over Uno house. And ain't no telling what we might run into."

With that said, Noni unzipped the bag and removed a AR-556 '300 Blackout'. An assault rifle equipped with a collapsible stock and green dot optic, Noni had replaced the standard clip for a 100-round drum— commonly known in the streets as a pair of 'Monkey Nuts'.

Forgetful of the text, Asha reversed out the driveway and made it to the end of the block, when one of her worse fears in life became a sudden reality.

Closing in on the Suburban as they had done with the dump truck, federal agents hopped out of unmarked vehicles with weapons resembling what Noni possessed. Warned that the suspects were likely armed and considerably dangerous, the agents took cover, sighted their weapons on the Suburban and yelled for the driver to cut off the ignition.

As Asha and Noni frantically searched for a possible means of escape, they saw they were surrounded. Masked men with tactical weapons were crouched beside houses and taking up cover behind parked cars. There was no way out.

Noni looked out her window, down at her rifle, then snatched back the slide and fed a cartridge to the chamber. With ninety-nine more in her drum, she was guaranteed to kill at least one. But she wouldn't go alone.

"Noni, stop it!" Asha said.

"Stop what? Girl, I can't let them put me in no cage for the rest of my life. Not when I can help it."

"But we don't even know what this is."

"Look how they came. This ain't no regular traffic stop."

"But what about me, Noni? What I'm supposed to do? Just watch them gun you down?"

"Twin, you been knew how I felt about not going back."

"Then who gon' watch over me and make sure I'm okay?"

"Asha, how I'ma do that if I'm locked up forever?"

"Because we'll go down together. As long as we got each other, it don't matter where we at. If you gotta do forever, I'll do forever with you. I'd rather have you like that, than not have you at all. But if your mind made up... then I'm going, too, Noni. You my twin, so we either gon' live together or die together."

Noni tearfully shook her head at the image of Asha being destroyed by a hail of bullets. She couldn't bear the thought of it. But neither could she bear the thought of doing a life sentence. And as her mind tried to reason that maybe this wasn't as serious as she assumed, her involvement in so many murders made that highly unlikely.

Asha sensed her sister's inner conflict and continued, "I know you can't see it right now, but we gon' be good, Noni. Everything gon' work in our favor. I haven't told you, but I've been praying every night. And it ain't no doubt in my mind God got us. He always has, we just never knew it. We've done some bad things, so I ain't saying we not gon' be punished. But I'm saying it's not gon' be as bad as you think."

At Asha's mention of God, Noni recalled the counsel she received from the lady Ms. Johnson— who owned the Rottweiler, Missy. *If you soon find yourself stuck in a undesirable situation, see it as a sign of affection from above. Because it says in the Bible, 'God disciplines those He loves'.*

As tears slid down her cheeks Noni softly confessed, "I'm scared, Asha."

"Me, too, love," Asha admitted. She wanted to hug her sister so bad, but didn't want the move to be mistaken as a threat by the federal agents.

At the sound of an overhead chopper, Asha reached over to take Noni's hand. "So what we gon' do?"

***

Angel leaned forward on her couch in suspense as she watched live footage of the twins traffic stop. Despite the Suburban being surrounded and a helicopter circling the scene, the suspects had yet to surrender.

"What the hell are they doing?" Angel mumbled to herself, wondering what the twins could possibly be doing inside the SUV.

Angel was the rat responsible for tipping off authorities to the dump truck move. Along with naming Noni as the leader of a drug operation, she said Noni had personally committed a number of murders— and that she was willing to testify if that's what it took to take a monster off the streets.

Angel turned up the volume at the sudden activity on the TV screen. Led by their weapons, FBI agents cautiously closed in on the Suburban. Then, as its doors simultaneously pushed open, the twins emerged from the truck, hands first in surrender.

Smiling in satisfaction, Angel watched agents take the twins into custody. She had executed her plan to perfection, and Noni would now pay the price for her negligent behavior. And in regard to Asha, she'd simply been a casualty of her sister's mistake.

Once the twins were transported from the scene, Angel went into the kitchen for a bottle of wine. She would toast to herself in the name of redemption. And while her family wouldn't approve of her dishonorable deed, it wasn't their heart that had been stolen and broken.

Chapter 20

A month after the twins were apprehended and booked into the Wayne County Jail, they were indicted on charges of felony drug trafficking, possession of a prohibited weapon—as Noni's assault rifle had been modified to a fully automatic, and three counts of aggravated murder. If convicted of all counts, they couldn't live long enough to see daylight again.

"I still can't believe she brought up them three bodies," Noni said as she sat at the foot of Asha's bed. They had learned from their lawyers that Angel was the state's star witness. "When she know—"

"Of course she know we ain't do it," Asha wisely cut her off, placing a finger to her lips for Noni to be quiet. For all she knew, there was a listening device somewhere in her room. "But you gotta understand she trying to protect her peoples. And she willing to throw us under the bus, if that's what it takes."

The three murders they were charged with stemmed from when they first met Perez. He was allegedly owed money by a dealer he supplied and offered the twins a seat at the table in exchange for taking the man's life. It just so happened that he never rode alone, forcing Noni to slaughter his security in the process.

Asha rose from the bed and went over to her door, where she peered out its window at the women in the dayroom. There were some on the phone; a lot watching TV; and others who stood in huddles, laughing and talking. But what most had in common was the look of contentment, and Asha couldn't help but wonder what had made them submit. A lot of those women were yet to be sentenced, but would rather crack jokes with strangers, than to go to the law library and work on their cases.

"What you over there thinking about?" Noni inquired.

"How this is all my fault," she answered, referring to the mishandling of the Angel situation. Asha had seen the signs of a scorned woman but had done nothing to address it.

"Why you say that?"

Before Asha could elaborate, their names were called for a visit over the pod's intercom. They checked each other's appearance to ensure it was on point, then put on their game face. Despite their situation's severity, they'd show no emotion.

Every eye in the pod seemed to stare at the twins as they exited the room. These were the two main members of the Butterfly Mafia— a notorious girl gang that held weight in the streets. They knew the pretty one was Asha; firm but fair. And the stud was Noni; a cold-hearted killer.

When the twins entered the visiting room, Shawna's face brightened behind the fiberglass partition. She snatched up the receiver in eagerness.

Because Noni was closest to the receiver on her and Asha's side, she picked it up and addressed Shawna first. "Girl, you gon' give yourself a whole heart attack, if you don't calm your happy-ass down."

"It's just so good to see y'all," Shawna smiled. "I know it's only been a month, but it feel more like forever."

Asha took the phone from her sister. "Don't listen to her, love, you know Noni mean. So how everything been going?"

Since the twins arrest, Asha did very little talking over the phones in the county. She knew a number of people whose own loose lips had sunken their ship, and she refused to drown herself in a similar manner.

Beginning with Big Baby's Daycare, Shawna informed them she now had a full staff and would open up soon. Club Skittles was doing bigger numbers, as Ray-Ray and Kiva continued to run it like real businesswomen. And there still hadn't been any news on Lo-Lo. "I don't know, Asha, it's like, her and that boy just up and disappeared."

Asha didn't know what to think, but right now she couldn't worry over what was beyond her control. "What about the weak link?" She asked in reference to Angel. "Any word on that?"

Shawna shook her head. Asha had written her a letter with instructions to contact Perez and inform him of his sister's violation of the street code. Shawna had left him a message but he'd yet to respond.

"Alright, don't worry about it," Asha said in comfort of Shawna's downcast expression. "Everything gon' work out, I just don't know how. And that's how God works. But you know what I really need from you?"

Shawna looked up with her dove-like eyes. "What?"

"I need you to hold it down, love. We started this together, so it's on you to keep the Butterfly Mafia alive. You in charge now. So it's time to see what them wings can do. We depending on you, Shawna."

"But what about Ray-Ray and Kiva? They are a lot older than me."

"This ain't got nothing to do with age. And besides, you've been through enough to make you strong as the next, if not stronger. You my baby sister, and I have faith in you, girl. You understand me? If anybody gon' take my spot, I want it to be you. So, do you got me, or what?"

Reflecting over everything Asha had done for her, Shawna knew there was no way she could let her girl down. It would be a tough role to fill, but it was time to face her fears and see if her wings worked. So she returned Asha's stare and assured her with all the confidence she had, "I got you, big sister. It's fly or die, and I can't help you if I'm dead. So I gotta make it happen."

Asha smiled at the maturity of her statement. Shawna was growing up and would undoubtedly transition into a sharp young lady.

"So what about posting bail?" Shawna asked. "I can put up the club and daycare as collateral."

"Nah, we gon' sit tight for a minute and fight this from the inside. It'll be better this way in the end, trust me."

When a guard announced visiting hours were over, Asha quickly ran off a list of things she wanted Shawna to do. "Tell Ray-Ray and Kiva I need them to come see me. Let Double-O know to drop off some more bread to his lil' dude's peoples. And, Shawna, I need you to stop by the Silverdome and pick up another present for our lawyers."

The Silverdome was the code word for the stash house in Pontiac, Michigan. With it's master bedroom still covered in currency, Asha wanted Shawna to scoop some up and drop it off to their lawyers. Because the twins didn't have adult felony records, the Feds declined jurisdiction and left their case on a state level— where the more money you spent, the less time you'd get.

Before parting ways, Asha pressed her hand to the glass and Shawna followed suit. "I love you," Asha mouthed, to which Shawna mouthed back, "I love you more."

Once Asha and Noni went through a door and disappeared out of her sight, it was then Shawna let a set of tears escape from her eyes.

***

Later that night Double-O and Shawna pulled into Club Skittles, where he parked the Porsche outside the front door. Shawna looked over her shoulder at Polaris— who played with Bella, and told her she'd be right back.

Inside the club, Ray-Ray, Kiva, and several other employees chilled in the backroom. The club was presently closed to the public, but this was where the women like to hang out at. While listening to music, they'd mix a little marijuana in with drinks and jokes.

"Wassup with the Mob?" They greeted as Shawna entered the room, rising to give her a genuine hug.

Replying she was good, Shawna declined the weed and liquor and stated the reason for her visit. "Asha want y'all to come see her as soon as possible."

"Alright, well, if you talk to her first, tell her we'll be down there tomorrow," Kiva said.

"And how they holding up?" Ray-Ray inquired, as Asha had yet to personally reach out.

"They optimistic," Shawna thought was the best word to describe their energy. "And you know, with them, it's like, as long as they got each other, they gon' get through whatever."

Ray-Ray nodded in agreement, as that was the definite truth. "Yeah, you ain't never lied. Because they definitely gotta hell of a bond. And I knew it was different by how they danced together on their birthday. That was some deep shit."

After the women fell silent in reflecting on the memory, Shawna shook it off to prevent growing emotional. It was time to step up, which would require more nerve. "Listen, I gotta run, and I'll see y'all tomorrow. But visiting hours with Asha start at noon."

As they watched Shawna leave, the women all noticed a difference in her demeanor. "Is it me?" Kiva said, "or did she just tell us we better have our asses down there tomorrow at noon?"

Ray-Ray laughed before sipping her drink. "Nah, she just definitely did. So you make sure you got your Puerto-Rican-ass down there tomorrow at 11:59."

When Shawna exited the club, a dark colored Dodge Ram rolled into the parking lot. Thinking it was the company of one of the girls inside, Shawna continued toward the car. But as she reached to open the door, the pickup stopped beside her and its passenger window lowered. "Excuse me, baby girl, but is this club still open?"

Despite being alarmed by his dangerous scent, Shawna calmly answered that it was, but not at the moment. "Unless it's booked for a private party or some other event, we only open up on Fridays and Saturdays."

"You said 'we'?" He readjusted himself in the seat. "Listen, not to be all up in your business, but is you one of the owners of this joint, or something?"

Double-O suddenly popped out the Porsche and stayed planted on the driver side. With a hand behind his back— which held on to a firearm, he tipped his head at the passenger in a gesture of peace. But the look in his cold, dark eyes conveyed a different message.

Emboldened by Double-O's presence, Shawna answered the man's question with one of her own. "Why, what's going on?"

He held up a folded wad of cash between two fingers. "I just need you to point me in the right direction."

Shawna couldn't believe her ears as he revealed what he needed. There was no way no one could've ever predicted it would unfold like this.

When Shawna and Double-O reentered the car, she looked over at him in sheer disbelief. "If I gave you a million tries, I bet you still couldn't guess who that was in that truck."

Chapter 21

It was the morning of Asha and Noni's trial date, and Angel got dressed in the bedroom of her new apartment. Shortly after their arrest, she had to change locations for safety purposes; for her brother no longer provided her with protection. But in spite of his anger over Angel's decision to become what he despised, she would do what it took to make sure Noni never returned to society.

Dressed to impress, Angel grabbed her purse, a pair of Ray Ban shades, and exited the apartment. As the state's star witness in the twins' joint trial, she would be taking the stand to give detailed testimony. Minus the part of her brother's involvement, she would explain to the jury how Noni had callously killed three men in broad day. And she would solidify her story by pointing out the scar on back of Noni's leg— where she'd been shot by the officer who pursued on that exact same day.

Cautious of her surroundings as she stepped outside, Angel noticed nothing suspicious on her way to the car. Her plan for today was to bury two things: Noni, and the past.

Inside her BMW coupe, Angel awakened the engine and reached for her seatbelt. She shrieked at the sudden shattering of her window. Before she had a chance to scramble or get a glimpse of her assailant, she was grabbed by the hair and roughly drug out the car. Thrown into the back of a gutted-out van, she opened her mouth to scream and was knocked unconscious.

Lying face down inside the moving van, Angel was initially confused as her eyes fluttered open. Then she recalled the kidnapping and turned over in panic. As panic instantly converted to absolute terror, Angel couldn't believe the identity of her evil-eyed assailant.

Crouched like a lion that was liable to leap, the kidnapper was a West Coast Crip whose street name was Bluefish Loc. And up front, the driver was his partner in crime, Big Feez.

Bluefish was the Crip from Compton who Angel had helped finesse out of $160,000. She had led him to believe she was the wife of a cartel captain. It had taken some time, but Bluefish had finally found her— thanks to the viral video of Noni's parking lot brawl with that man outside the club. Angel was present that night and her face had been captured in the video. From there it was just a matter of Bluefish and Feez taking a trip to Detroit. And with luck on their side, they had bumped into Shawna that night outside Skittles; and she just so happened to know who Angel was.

Angel couldn't believe it. The women she hated— who sat safely in jail, would ultimately be the cause of her death. And she knew it was no one's fault but her own. Because had she just left it alone and moved on, she would've still had the security team her brother provided.

"You know what you did, and I'm only gon' ask you once," Bluefish warned, cracking his knuckles and stretching his neck." Bitch, where the fuck is my money?"

***

Inside a packed courtroom— where nearly all the attendants were women in support of the twins, Asha and Noni sat at the defense table with their team of high-powered female attorneys. Whereas the defendants appeared to be calm, the prosecution side were running around like headless chickens. They had a crisis on their hands— and it involved the absence of their key witness, Angel.

"Your Honor, may I approach the bench?" The twins lead counsel, Ms. Roman, requested, to which the judge waved her forward. "You may, counselor."

With the prosecutor also present in the huddle, Ms. Roman stated, "Your Honor, as we know, my clients are entitled to their speedy trial rights, and we're ready to proceed. The trial was scheduled to commence at 9 a.m. sharp, and it's now 9:30. Both sides have had ample amount of time to prepare their cases, so I say, let's put rubber to the ground and get this thing rolling."

Desperate for a continuance, the prosecutor pled to the judge, "Your Honor, our witness is suddenly nowhere to be found. I just spoke with her last night, so there's reason to believe there may be foul play involved."

"On whose end?" Ms. Roman asked in indignity. "Because as we know, my clients have been in custody since their arrest, and I'm sure you're aware they rarely talk on the phone. So if foul play is involved, you might like to look into your witness's family— who are buried neck deep in illegal activities."

The judge pondered a moment, then placed a palm over the microphone and spoke to the prosecutor. "I understand your position, but I can't grant a continuance based on a hunch. So unless you can provide proof of witness tampering, then, counselor, I'm afraid you'll have to proceed with your case."

The prosecutor dropped his head in defeat, for his entire case rested on Angel's testimony. The two juvenile boys who'd been caught with the drugs were claiming sole ownership. But there was still the weapons charge. "Your Honor, excuse me while I have a brief word with my assistant."

After whispering back and forth with his female assistant, the prosecutor returned to the bench with a proposal. "If the defendants are willing to accept, the state is prepared to offer a 2-year plea deal on the weapons charge. If not, we can take it to trial and see which story the jury likes more."

When Ms. Roman returned to the defense table and told them the offer, Asha closed her eyes in genuine gratitude; for this was God granting them a second chance at life, for her a third.

Without a need to discuss it, Asha looked up at Ms. Roman and smiled, "Where do we sign?"

Once the judge went on record and sentenced the defendants to 24 months in the Michigan Department of Corrections, the courtroom erupted in cheers as Asha and Noni fiercely embraced.

"I told you we'd be good," Asha whispered to her sister before kissing her cheek.

As they were led from the courtroom, the twins paused in surprise at the sight of their father. "I'm just rooting from afar," he held up his hands in an innocent gesture.

Asha's cordial response gave him a glimmer of hope. "Yeah, well, I guess ain't nothing wrong with that."

Next, they saw Ray-Ray and Kiva— who were fashionably fitted and wore a BFM chain. "You know what they said when they cut the dog's tail off," Kiva smiled. "...It won't be long now. See y'all in a minute, love."

Last but not least, they locked eyes with Shawna— the girl who had flew through and saved the day. They had once rescued her when she was down on her luck, and she returned the favor when it mattered the most.

With their love for each other self-explanatory, Asha simply patted her heart, which was where Shawna lived. "For life!"

Chapter 22

3 months later...

In a champagne-colored Jeep Wagoneer, Double-O did the speed limit down I-75. Beside him was Shawna, who earnestly scribbled on some type of postcard. And in the backseat was Polaris and Bella, who were both currently asleep. With a long drive ahead, they were en route to a place every child wished to go— Disney Land. Polaris had recently turned six, and this was just one of her many birthday gifts.

A lot had happened over the course of three months. For starters, Big Baby's Daycare had opened and was an instant success. To help cleanse some of the money at the stash house in Pontiac, Shawna offered free daycare services for the first sixty days; and would cover the expenses on paper herself.

Club Skittles was officially the hottest spot in the city, where dancers were recruited from all over the Midwest. But despite their success, Ray-Ray and Kiva respected Asha's wishes on leaving Shawna in charge. And their philosophy was simple: there was no place for envy when the food was plenty.

Lo-Lo's disappearance still remained a mystery, though there were rumors that her and Uno had been buried alive. If she had listened, Shawna often thought to herself.

"Alright, I'm ready," Shawna told Double-O once she finished with the postcard.

He got off on the next exit and located a mailbox. Shawna lowered her window, checked to make sure she addressed the postcard correctly, then leaned to stick it through the mailbox opening. She smiled to herself as the Jeep pulled off.

They were driving through Kentucky, when Polaris woke up.

After looking down at Bella, then out at the passing scenery, Polaris spoke six words that brought Shawna to tears, "Mama, can we stop at McDonald's?"

***

Huron Valley Complex...

Serving their sentence at a prison in Ypsilanti, Michigan, Asha and Noni confidently strode through a yard full of women. Coming from the recreation building, their sweat-soaked clothing was evidence of the intense workout they had just completed. They could be released on good behavior by the following year, and Noni had every intention on returning to the ring; which meant it was mandatory she stayed in shape.

Though they kept a low profile and stuck to themselves, word eventually got out they were top-ranking members of the Butterfly Mafia. A handful hated, but the majority paid homage in hopes of being recruited.

"So is you ready for this test?" Asha asked Noni as they cut across the compound. Asha had enrolled them both in GED classes.

"Yeah, I'm ready," Noni answered in a halfhearted tone. "But I still don't see what the point of it is."

"Because we grown-ass woman, that's the point. And if we can put our minds to accomplishing what we did in the streets, then clearly we can put our minds to getting our GED. So you better be studying. Because I'm telling you right now, Noni, I'm not letting you cheat off me. The same way you gotta go in that ring and earn that win, is the same way you gotta go in that classroom and earn that certificate. You hear me, girl?"

"I'm too near you not to," Noni retorted.

"Alright." Asha playfully nudged her. "With your smart-ass. Think it's game if you want to."

Asha's mouth said one thing, but she knew in her heart she'd do whatever it took to see her sister succeed. She was just pushing her to be prosperous in her spectrum of life. While their sentence was undoubtedly a slap on the wrist, Asha wouldn't take the blessing for granted by not sharpening her sword. And because Noni's existence was as precious as her own, Asha would ensure that she also returned to society with a sharper perspective.

Upon entering their housing unit, the female guard on duty waved them over to her desk. "Here's your mail," she handed it to Asha, slipping Noni a look like she'd eat her alive.

"Oooh, let me find out you hitting Big Bertha!" Asha joked with her sister as they went to their room.

"I'm saying," Noni smiled, flashing her flawless VVS's, "It ain't like right now I wouldn't. Shit, in certain situations, you gotta take one for the team, you feel me?"

Inside their room— where they lived together, Asha fondly smiled at the postcard from Shawna. She turned it over and read out loud:

"Dear Big Sisters... I love y'all more right now than I did last night, and I'll love you even more if I live to see tomorrow. Thank you for seeing in me what I didn't see in myself. And for that, my loyalty is yours for as long as I breathe. Because is not our crowning principle, By L.O.V.E. We Abide? And is not the definition of love, L.oyalty O.utweighs V.irtually E.verything?

BFM for life!

Your sister's keeper, Shawna."

With goosebumps on her arms as she finished reading the postcard, Asha looked up at her twin and broadly grinned, "Long Live The Mob!"

Chapter 23

A LETTER TO LEROY pt.2

My last question was could you imagine the hurdles I encountered on account of your cowardly actions?... Or the pain I sustained while searching for someone to replace your absence?

Did you know that when others would harshly condemn you, my loyalty I'd lend you and readily defend you?... If you would've gotten to know me, you would've known all I wanted was to love and befriend you.

And perhaps my perception of love was improper because of your willful neglect... And yes, I once thought sex was the way for a couple to fully connect.

You forced me to fend for myself in a world where mercy is rarely extended... And that period when I yearned for your praise and approval has finally ended.

And though I could never forget you, due to our sharing a likeness in features... I could never forgive you, for you failed to fulfill your role as my teacher.

As I scribbled these words, my friends would all ask, "why even bother?"... And it's because your cruelty created a Queen, so I had to say thank you for being a deadbeat father.

Fumiya Payne.

Lock Down Publications and Ca$h Presents
Assisted Publishing Packages

BASIC PACKAGE	UPGRADED PACKAGE
$499	$800
Editing	Typing
Cover Design	Editing
Formatting	Cover Design
	Formatting
ADVANCE PACKAGE	**LDP SUPREME PACKAGE**
$1,200	$1,500
Typing	Typing
Editing	Editing
Cover Design	Cover Design
Formatting	Formatting
Copyright registration	Copyright registration
Proofreading	Proofreading
Upload book to Amazon	Set up Amazon account
	Upload book to Amazon
	Advertise on LDP, Amazon and Facebook Page

***Other services available upon request.
Additional charges may apply

Lock Down Publications
P.O. Box 944
Stockbridge, GA 30281-9998
Phone: 470 303-9761

Submission Guideline

Submit the first three chapters of your completed manuscript to ldpsubmissions@gmail.com. In the subject line add **Your Book's Title**. The manuscript must be in a Word Doc file and sent as an attachment. Document should be in Times New Roman, double spaced, and in size 12 font. Also, provide your synopsis and full contact information. If sending multiple submissions, they must each be in a separate email.

Have a story but no way to send it electronically? You can still submit to LDP/Ca$h Presents. Send in the first three chapters, written or typed, of your completed manuscript to:

LDP: Submissions Dept
P.O. Box 944
Stockbridge, GA 30281-9998

DO NOT send original manuscript. Must be a duplicate. Provide your synopsis and a cover letter containing your full contact information.

Thanks for considering LDP and Ca$h Presents.

NEW RELEASES

BLOODLINE OF A SAVAGE 1&2
THESE VICIOUS STREETS 1&2
RELENTLESS GOON
RELENTLESS GOON 2
BY PRINCE A. TAUHID

THE BUTTERFLY MAFIA 1-3
BY FUMIYA PAYNE

A THUG'S STREET PRINCESS 1&2
BY MEESHA

CITY OF SMOKE 2
BY MOLOTTI

STEPPERS 1,2&3
THE REAL BADDIES OF CHI-RAQ
BY KING RIO

THE LANE 1&2
BY KEN-KEN SPENCE

THUG OF SPADES 1&2
LOVE IN THE TRENCHES 2
CORNER BOYS
BY COREY ROBINSON

TIL DEATH 3
BY ARYANNA

THE BIRTH OF A GANGSTER 4
BY DELMONT PLAYER

PRODUCT OF THE STREETS 1&2
BY DEMOND "MONEY" ANDERSON

NO TIME FOR ERROR
BY KEESE

MONEY HUNGRY DEMONS
BY TRANAY ADAMS

Coming Soon from Lock Down Publications/Ca$h Presents

IF YOU CROSS ME ONCE 6
ANGEL V
By Anthony Fields

IMMA DIE BOUT MINE 5
By Aryanna

A THUGS STREET PRINCESS 3
By Meesha

PRODUCT OF THE STREETS 3
By Demond Money Anderson

CORNER BOYS 2
By Corey Robinson

THE MURDER QUEENS 6&7
By Michael Gallon

CITY OF SMOKE 3
By Molotti

CONFESSIONS OF A DOPE BOY
By Nicholas Lock

THA TAKEOVER
By Keith Chandler

BETRAYAL OF A G 2
By Ray Vinci

CRIME BOSS
By Playa Ray

Available Now

RESTRAINING ORDER 1 & 2
By **CA$H & Coffee**

LOVE KNOWS NO BOUNDARIES 1-3
By **Coffee**

RAISED AS A GOON I, II, III & IV
BRED BY THE SLUMS I, II, III
BLAST FOR ME I & II
ROTTEN TO THE CORE I II III
A BRONX TALE I, II, III
DUFFLE BAG CARTEL I II III IV V VI
HEARTLESS GOON I II III IV V
A SAVAGE DOPEBOY I II
DRUG LORDS I II III
CUTTHROAT MAFIA I II
KING OF THE TRENCHES
By **Ghost**

LAY IT DOWN I & II
LAST OF A DYING BREED I II
BLOOD STAINS OF A SHOTTA I & II III
By **Jamaica**

LOYAL TO THE GAME I II III
LIFE OF SIN I, II III
By **TJ & Jelissa**

IF LOVING HIM IS WRONG…I & II
LOVE ME EVEN WHEN IT HURTS I II III
By **Jelissa**

PUSH IT TO THE LIMIT
By **Bre' Hayes**

BLOODY COMMAS I & II
SKI MASK CARTEL I, II & III
KING OF NEW YORK I II, III IV V
RISE TO POWER I II III
COKE KINGS I II III IV V
BORN HEARTLESS I II III IV
KING OF THE TRAP I II
By **T.J. Edwards**

WHEN THE STREETS CLAP BACK I & II III
THE HEART OF A SAVAGE I II III IV
MONEY MAFIA I II
LOYAL TO THE SOIL I II III
By **Jibril Williams**

A DISTINGUISHED THUG STOLE MY HEART I II & III
LOVE SHOULDN'T HURT I II III IV
RENEGADE BOYS 1-4
PAID IN KARMA 1-3
SAVAGE STORMS 1-3
AN UNFORESEEN LOVE 1-3
BABY, I'M WINTERTIME COLD 1-3
A THUG'S STREET PRINCESS 1&2
By **Meesha**

A GANGSTER'S CODE 1-3
A GANGSTER'S SYN 1-3
THE SAVAGE LIFE 1-3
CHAINED TO THE STREETS 1-3
BLOOD ON THE MONEY 1-3
A GANGSTA'S PAIN 1-3
BEAUTIFUL LIES AND UGLY TRUTHS
CHURCH IN THESE STREETS
By **J-Blunt**

CUM FOR ME 1-8
An LDP Erotica Collaboration

BLOOD OF A BOSS 1-5
SHADOWS OF THE GAME
TRAP BASTARD
By **Askari**

THE STREETS BLEED MURDER 1-3
THE HEART OF A GANGSTA 1-3
By **Jerry Jackson**

WHEN A GOOD GIRL GOES BAD
By **Adrienne**

THE COST OF LOYALTY 1-3
By **Kweli**

BRIDE OF A HUSTLA 1-3
THE FETTI GIRLS 1-3
CORRUPTED BY A GANGSTA 1-4
BLINDED BY HIS LOVE
THE PRICE YOU PAY FOR LOVE 1-3
DOPE GIRL MAGIC 1-3
By **Destiny Skai**

A KINGPIN'S AMBITION
A KINGPIN'S AMBITION II
I MURDER FOR THE DOUGH
By **Ambitious**

TRUE SAVAGE 1-7
DOPE BOY MAGIC 1-3
MIDNIGHT CARTEL 1-3
CITY OF KINGZ 1&2
NIGHTMARE ON SILENT AVE
THE PLUG OF LIL MEXICO 1&2
CLASSIC CITY
By **Chris Green**

A GANGSTER'S REVENGE 1-4
THE BOSS MAN'S DAUGHTERS 1-5
A SAVAGE LOVE 1&2
BAE BELONGS TO ME 1&2
A HUSTLER'S DECEIT 1-3
WHAT BAD BITCHES DO 1-3
SOUL OF A MONSTER 1-3
KILL ZONE
A DOPE BOY'S QUEEN 1-3
TIL DEATH 1-3
IMMA DIE BOUT MINE 1-4
By **Aryanna**

A DOPEBOY'S PRAYER
By **Eddie "Wolf" Lee**

THE KING CARTEL 1-3
By **Frank Gresham**

THESE NIGGAS AIN'T LOYAL 1-3
By **Nikki Tee**

GANGSTA SHYT 1-3
By **CATO**

THE ULTIMATE BETRAYAL
By **Phoenix**

BOSS'N UP 1-3
By **Royal Nicole**

I LOVE YOU TO DEATH
By **Destiny J**

I RIDE FOR MY HITTA
I STILL RIDE FOR MY HITTA
By **Misty Holt**

LOVE & CHASIN' PAPER
By **Qay Crockett**

TO DIE IN VAIN
SINS OF A HUSTLA
By **ASAD**

BROOKLYN HUSTLAZ
By **Boogsy Morina**

BROOKLYN ON LOCK 1 & 2
By **Sonovia**

GANGSTA CITY
By **Teddy Duke**

A DRUG KING AND HIS DIAMOND 1-3
A DOPEMAN'S RICHES
HER MAN, MINE'S TOO 1&2
CASH MONEY HO'S
THE WIFEY I USED TO BE 1&2
PRETTY GIRLS DO NASTY THINGS
By **Nicole Goosby**

LIPSTICK KILLAH 1-3
CRIME OF PASSION 1-3
FRIEND OR FOE 1-3
By **Mimi**

TRAPHOUSE KING 1-3
KINGPIN KILLAZ 1-3
STREET KINGS 1&2
PAID IN BLOOD 1&2
CARTEL KILLAZ 1-3
DOPE GODS 1&2
By **Hood Rich**

THE STREETS ARE CALLING
By **Duquie Wilson**

STEADY MOBBN' 1-3
THE STREETS STAINED MY SOUL 1-3
By **Marcellus Allen**

WHO SHOT YA 1-3
SON OF A DOPE FIEND 1-4
HEAVEN GOT A GHETTO 1&2
SKI MASK MONEY 1&2
By **Renta**

GORILLAZ IN THE BAY 1-4
TEARS OF A GANGSTA 1/&2
3X KRAZY 1&2
STRAIGHT BEAST MODE 1&2
By **DE'KARI**

TRIGGADALE 1-3
MURDA WAS THE CASE 1-3
By **Elijah R. Freeman**

SLAUGHTER GANG 1-3
RUTHLESS HEART 1-3
By **Willie Slaughter**

GOD BLESS THE TRAPPERS 1-3
THESE SCANDALOUS STREETS 1-3
FEAR MY GANGSTA 1-5
THESE STREETS DON'T LOVE NOBODY 1-2
BURY ME A G 1-5
A GANGSTA'S EMPIRE 1-4
THE DOPEMAN'S BODYGAURD 1&2
THE REALEST KILLAZ 1-3
THE LAST OF THE OGS 1-3
By **Tranay Adams**

MARRIED TO A BOSS 1-3
By **Destiny Skai & Chris Green**

KINGZ OF THE GAME 1-7
CRIME BOSS 1-3
By **Playa Ray**

FUK SHYT
By **Blakk Diamond**

DON'T F#CK WITH MY HEART 1&2
By **Linnea**

ADDICTED TO THE DRAMA 1-3
IN THE ARM OF HIS BOSS
By **Jamila**

LOYALTY AIN'T PROMISED 1&2
By **Keith Williams**

YAYO 1-4
A SHOOTER'S AMBITION 1&2
BRED IN THE GAME
By **S. Allen**

TRAP GOD 1-3
RICH $AVAGE 1-3
MONEY IN THE GRAVE 1-3
CARTEL MONEY
By **Martell Troublesome Bolden**

FOREVER GANGSTA 1&2
GLOCKS ON SATIN SHEETS 1&2
By **Adrian Dulan**

TOE TAGZ 1-4
LEVELS TO THIS SHYT 1&2
IT'S JUST ME AND YOU
By **Ah'Million**

KINGPIN DREAMS 1-3
RAN OFF ON DA PLUG
By **Paper Boi Rari**

THE STREETS MADE ME 1-3
By **Larry D. Wright**

CONFESSIONS OF A GANGSTA 1-4
CONFESSIONS OF A JACKBOY 1-3
CONFESSIONS OF A HITMAN
By **Nicholas Lock**

I'M NOTHING WITHOUT HIS LOVE
SINS OF A THUG
TO THE THUG I LOVED BEFORE
A GANGSTA SAVED XMAS
IN A HUSTLER I TRUST
By **Monet Dragun**

QUIET MONEY 1-3
THUG LIFE 1-3
EXTENDED CLIP 1&2
A GANGSTA'S PARADISE
By **Trai'Quan**

CAUGHT UP IN THE LIFE 1-3
THE STREETS NEVER LET GO 1-3
By **Robert Baptiste**

NEW TO THE GAME 1-3
MONEY, MURDER & MEMORIES 1-3
By **Malik D. Rice**

CREAM 2-3
THE STREETS WILL TALK
By **Yolanda Moore**

THE STREETS WILL NEVER CLOSE 1-3
By **K'ajji**

LIFE OF A SAVAGE 1-4
A GANGSTA'S QUR'AN 1-4
MURDA SEASON 1-3
GANGLAND CARTEL 1-3
CHI'RAQ GANGSTAS 1-4
KILLERS ON ELM STREET 1-3
JACK BOYZ N DA BRONX 1-3
A DOPEBOY'S DREAM 1-3
JACK BOYS VS DOPE BOYS 1-3
COKE GIRLZ
COKE BOYS
SOSA GANG 1&2
BRONX SAVAGES
BODYMORE KINGPINS
BLOOD OF A GOON
By **Romell Tukes**

CONCRETE KILLA 1-3
VICIOUS LOYALTY 1-3
By **Kingpen**

THE ULTIMATE SACRIFICE 1-6
KHADIFI
IF YOU CROSS ME ONCE 1-3
ANGEL 1-4
IN THE BLINK OF AN EYE
By **Anthony Fields**

THE LIFE OF A HOOD STAR
By **Ca$h & Rashia Wilson**

NIGHTMARES OF A HUSTLA 1-3
BLOOD AND GAMES 1&2
By **King Dream**

GHOST MOB
By **Stilloan Robinson**

HARD AND RUTHLESS 1&2
MOB TOWN 251
THE BILLIONAIRE BENTLEYS 1-3
REAL G'S MOVE IN SILENCE
By **Von Diesel**

MOB TIES 1-7
SOUL OF A HUSTLER, HEART OF A KILLER 1-3
GORILLAZ IN THE TRENCHES
By **SayNoMore**

BODYMORE MURDERLAND 1-3
THE BIRTH OF A GANGSTER 1-4
By **Delmont Player**

FOR THE LOVE OF A BOSS 1&2
By **C. D. Blue**

KILLA KOUNTY 1-5
By **Khufu**

MOBBED UP 1-4
THE BRICK MAN 1-5
THE COCAINE PRINCESS 1-10
STEPPERS 1-3
SUPER GREMLIN 1-4
By **King Rio**

MONEY GAME 1&2
By **Smoove Dolla**

A GANGSTA'S KARMA 1-4
By **FLAME**

KING OF THE TRENCHES 1-3
By **GHOST & TRANAY ADAMS**

THE BUTTERFLY MAFIA 4 | FUMIYA PAYNE

QUEEN OF THE ZOO 1&2
By **Black Migo**

GRIMEY WAYS 1-3
BETRAYAL OF A G
By **Ray Vinci**

XMAS WITH AN ATL SHOOTER
By **Ca$h & Destiny Skai**

KING KILLA 1&2
By **Vincent "Vitto" Holloway**

BETRAYAL OF A THUG 1&2
By **Fre$h**

THE MURDER QUEENS 1-5
By **Michael Gallon**

FOR THE LOVE OF BLOOD 1-4
By **Jamel Mitchell**

HOOD CONSIGLIERE 1&2
NO TIME FOR ERROR
By **Keese**

PROTÉGÉ OF A LEGEND 1&2
LOVE IN THE TRENCHES 1&2
By **Corey Robinson**

THE PLUG'S RUTHLESS DAUGHTER
By **Tony Daniels**

BORN IN THE GRAVE 1-3
CRIME PAYS
By **Self Made Tay**

MOAN IN MY MOUTH
By **XTASY**

TORN BETWEEN A GANGSTER AND A GENTLEMAN
By **J-BLUNT & Miss Kim**

LOYALTY IS EVERYTHING 1-3
CITY OF SMOKE 1&2
By **Molotti**

HERE TODAY GONE TOMORROW 1&2
By **Fly Rock**

WOMEN LIE MEN LIE 1-4
FIFTY SHADES OF SNOW 1-3
STACK BEFORE YOU SPLURGE
GIRLS FALL LIKE DOMINOES
NAÏVE TO THE STREETS
By **ROY MILLIGAN**

PILLOW PRINCESS
By **S. Hawkins**

THE BUTTERFLY MAFIA 1-3
SALUTE MY SAVAGERY 1&2
By **Fumiya Payne**

THE LANE 1&2
By Ken-Ken Spence

THE PUSSY TRAP 1-5
By **Nene Capri**

DIRTY DNA
By **Blaque**

SANCTIFIED AND HORNY
by **XTASY**

BOOKS BY LDP'S CEO, CA$H

TRUST IN NO MAN
TRUST IN NO MAN 2
TRUST IN NO MAN 3
BONDED BY BLOOD
SHORTY GOT A THUG
THUGS CRY
THUGS CRY 2
THUGS CRY 3
TRUST NO BITCH
TRUST NO BITCH 2
TRUST NO BITCH 3
TIL MY CASKET DROPS
RESTRAINING ORDER
RESTRAINING ORDER 2
IN LOVE WITH A CONVICT
LIFE OF A HOOD STAR
XMAS WITH AN ATL SHOOTER

www.ingramcontent.com/pod-product-compliance
Lightning Source LLC
Chambersburg PA
CBHW070523260626
47161CB00004B/1620